# VENGEANCE AT AULIS
## A *Trojan Murders* Mystery


Peter Tonkin

For:
Cham, Guy, Mark and Lana as always.

# CONTENTS

# 1 - The Contest on the Beach

i

'So,' said my father, 'tell me about your captain's women.'

'For Odysseus there is only one woman,' I answered. 'His wife Penelope is *the* woman as far as he's concerned. Why do you ask?'

'Apparently there is one looking for him. A mysterious woman of great beauty, though how she hopes to find him as things stand at the moment only the gods know.' He lifted his arm in a sweeping gesture that covered the entire fifty-thousand-man army gathered here in one massive camp and the thousand ships in the bay beside them. 'Or why she wants to find him, come to that.'

'I'm sure she'll be trying to find him so that he can help her with some problem. He's adept at solving riddles,' I explained. Then I added, for emphasis, 'and he's faithful to his wife.'

'As his rhapsode you'd know, of course.' Father nodded. 'However, some of his friends seem to be less single-minded,' he continued. 'Take young Prince Achilles for instance. I hear he's left Princess Deidamia of Skyros behind in Phthia, pregnant with his baby and with Queen Thetis his mother keeping a close eye on her.'

'Where did you hear that?' I wondered, labouring to keep up with his purposeful stride as well as with this flow of information.

We were walking along a pathway that followed the shore, between the tidemark and the lines of the army's huge encampment. It had been beaten hard by countless feet. On our left stood low dunes held together by coarse sea-grass; both the grass and the sand blown towards us by the easterly wind gusting in off the bay. The dunes slowly yielded to a stony beach that sloped down to the water's edge where the white surf tumbled out of a grey sea. A seemingly endless line of ships had been driven ashore here, starting with those commanded by Prince Ajax of Salamis and ending in the far

1

distance with the black ships of the Myrmidons led by
Achilles, Prince of Phthia. Each vessel was further anchored
by hawsers reaching from their foredecks to stakes
hammered into the ground, just on the sea-side of the ridge
of solid sand that ran the length or the beach.

On our right was a temporary tent-city of linen and leather
that stretched as far inland as the hillslopes with their tall pine
forests filled with groves that were sacred to various gods
and goddesses, most especially to Artemis upon whose
protection the continued safety and prosperity of the local
area relied. Behind us stood the southern walls of the port
city of Aulis that we called home. Ahead of us was a huge
crowd of soldiers so bored with enforced inactivity that
almost any diversion called forth wild enthusiasm. Above it
all a low grey sky heavy with rainclouds being pushed
westward by a relentless and unseasonable north-easterly
gale.

'Where did I hear it? The same place as I heard about the
woman looking for Odysseus: *around*.' Father flung the last
word over his shoulder, glancing back as he did so. Then,
seeing how hard it was for me to keep up with him even on
the firm, flat pathway, he moderated his pace and continued
his explanation more slowly too. 'It's gossip on the docks. I
keep my ear to the ground and employ others to do so on my
behalf – good business practise. The rumour about Prince
Achilles and the child he's already fathered suggests that the
princess wasn't really what you'd call willing but he was
hiding in disguise among her women and she found that she
just couldn't say *no*.' He shrugged, then continued, 'some of
the others leave even less room for doubt and debate. Take
Prince Aias of Locris, for instance. He might be a brave
soldier but when it comes to women, he's almost insatiable
and likes things rough; he'd rather rape them than romance
them. And as for Prince Palamedes…'

My father's voice drifted away as he became lost in
thought. I would have found it difficult to hear much more in

2

any case because we were nearing our destination. The crowd of excited soldiers we were approaching were shouting at one-another; making wagers for the most part. Which was why we were here. To wager. I might be the closest of my father's sons behind him as we walked and talked, but behind me were several of my brothers, all laden with ornaments, trinkets, weapons and armour suitable to be wagered when the competition began.

\*\*\*

My father's business took in any element from which he could make a profit and, indeed, it was among the most profitable in the port city of Aulis. Together with his partners in the nearby harbour of Chalcis, he ran a vast trading empire centred on the two ports but stretching from Phonecian Tyre in the east to the Gates of Gades in the west – which people were beginning to call the Pillars of Hercules these days. From the fabled port of Colchis in the north, past Troy at the narrows where the Sea of Marmara flowed into the Aegean, to Crete and Egypt in the south. It was Troy which I knew best, every alleyway, hostel, temple and agora marketplace from the docks to King Priam's citadel. Well-founded, high-walled Troy, where I had been robbed and beaten almost to death, leaving me crippled, half blind and lucky to be able to scrape a living as a rhapsode, singing pastorals and epics accompanied by my lyre. Blessed by the gods in that I was rhapsode to Odysseus, King of Ithaca.

So it transpired that the least and most damaged of my father's family was the one he paid most attention to when I was visiting my home. For in my travels with Captain Odysseus, I met kings and princes, captains and generals: the men with whom Father wished to trade, especially as all the richest and most powerful were assembled here, in and around Aulis, waiting to set sail for Troy as soon as the weather changed. But the unseasonable easterly gales had settled in a few days ago and showed no sign of moderating any time soon. None of the local oracles seemed able or willing to explain why the weather had turned bad or when it was likely to improve. Even the army's chief seer the soothsayer Kalkhas could offer nothing much in the way of guidance.

The presence of High King Agamemnon, ruler of Mycenae, and his vast army trapped on the plains outside the city presented my father with a huge source of further profit; one that should have sufficed. But no: he was apparently considering whether he should supply women to the troops as well as food and drink. And he was planning to do that as soon as he could send his ships to the slave market in Ephesus. In the mean-time, he was adding to his revenue by making and accepting wagers when there were contests worthy of his notice. And that was the case now, for Prince Achilles was proposing to race on foot against a chariot pulled by four fast horses driven by Eumelos, one of the greatest charioteers in the whole of Achaea. Moreover, was planning to run the course in full armour; the golden armour that clothed him from head to foot when he went into battle. If the prince lost, the armour was Eumelos'; if the charioteer lost, his chariot and horses belonged to the prince. That was the way we made our simple wagers in those days.

'And you think Achilles will win?' Father called back suddenly. 'It doesn't seem likely, no matter how fast he is. Not in heavy golden armour against a chariot pulled by four horses. You're certain, boy? There could be a lot riding on it.'

'I'm certain of nothing,' I answered. 'Except I know that Captain Odysseus is sure he will win.'

The conversation was enough to take us to the starting line. The crowd here was thickest, but Father had no trouble in pushing through to the front. I and my brothers followed him. 'Who wishes to wager?' Father shouted, his voice surprisingly piercing in the blustery storm wind. A group of men standing a little apart from the soldiers and sailors swung round. I recognised the solid, square figure of my captain King Odysseus with the sprightly if elderly King Nestor of Pylos standing beside him, and beyond Nestor, Odysseus' closest friend and greatest enemy side by side – Diomedes, his companion from youth and Palamedes who had seen through his attempt to avoid joining he Trojan campaign and told Agamemnon of his trick. The trick had been to pretend madness and it had worked perfectly until the officious Palamedes had put Odysseus' baby son Telemachus in danger so the king was forced to admit the truth or to kill his own child; an act that was, of course, utterly unthinkable to any sane man.

'I wager that Prince Achilles will win!' called my father. 'Who will bet against me, like for like?'

My brothers spread cloths on the ground and displayed what we had brought; almost all of it designed to catch the eye and tempt the hearts of the soldiers.

'Welcome, lad,' said Odysseus as he crossed towards us, leading the others of his little group.

'Good morning, Captain,' I said. 'My father tells me he has heard of a mysterious woman searching for you. He says she is very beautiful.'

'Really?' answered Odysseus. 'That's news to me. Perhaps I will start looking for her after our business here is concluded. I see you have convinced your father to bet on the underdog.' He gestured and I looked up.

ii

Across the width of the beach the two contestants were going through their final preparations. Except that there were really six contestants, for Eumelos was quietening the four strong horses that would pull his chariot. The four steeds stood shoulder to shoulder, the central pair harnessed to the pole and the outer pair to a trace, all of their tack covered in jewels held fast in place by bands of gold. The chariot itself was a light carriage, made of wicker and woven leather edged and decorated in gold, the only weight or solidity lay in the planks of the base which sat above the axle joining wheels whose upper rims reached as high as the charioteer's hip. On the far side of the beach-floored course, Patroclus, Achilles' closest companion, was tightening the straps on the golden cuirass that bound his friend's chest as Achilles himself put his helmet on. Achilles' hair was a riot of golden strands that seemed to blaze even in the dull daylight. When he put on his golden helmet, it was as though he was snuffing out a candle flame. With his helm firmly in place, its scarlet plume blowing in the bluster, he reached for his shield. Patroclus pulled it out of his grasp, however. Achilles glanced across at Eumelos who met his gaze and simply shrugged. It seemed that he was not too worried whether Achilles took his shield or not. Achilles shrugged in turn and nodded. Patroclus put the shield away. Achilles swung round to face the track he was to follow along the beach. He was ready.

'So,' said Odysseus as he arrived at my side, 'what convinced you I was right?'

'The fact that you said it, Captain,' I answered.

Diomedes, at Odysseus' shoulder gave a bark of laughter. 'Blind faith!' he chuckled.

'Faith indeed,' nodded Odysseus. 'But he's neither as blind or as crippled as he looks. You should never underestimate my rhapsode, old friend. So, lad, have you worked out how he's going to pull it off?' He dropped his voice and glanced beyond me to where King Nestor and Prince Palamedes were heading a queue of men eager to wager some of their most precious possessions on the belief that Achilles was going to lose.

'He's the fastest man in the High King's army,' I said, my tone uncertain.

'Don't let him hear you say that,' advised my captain. 'He and the Myrmidons are fighting *with* the army, not as a part *of* the army. The High King may request that Achilles do something but he can never order him to do it. It's a question of pride and honour – and Achilles is the personification of

6

both. But the lad's no fool, and unlike Eumelos, he's not overconfident. He's relying on more than fleetness of foot today. After we watch him win, I'll tell you how he did it if you haven't worked it out for yourself by that time. And, from the look of things I'll have to lend you a couple of my crewmen to help your father carry his winnings home.'

We had to wait for longer than I expected but that was my father's fault. There were even some Myrmidons keen to bet against their commander. But at last the final wager was agreed and Patroclus called on Nestor as the senior leader there to start the race. My interest further piqued by my captain's implied challenge, I focussed on the proceedings with all my attention.

The course had been selected, measured and laid out by Achilles who, with Patroclus, had seemingly approached the matter as though they were preparing for a battle – much to Eumelos' apparent amusement. The race was to be run over a course that was almost a dolichos in length; marked by ten posts, each at the end of a two-hundred pace stadion. The entire course, therefore was two thousand paces, four hundred paces short of a full dolichos. Each stadion was marked by a post beside which stood a Myrmidon ready to call out the name of whoever was in the lead as they came past. The path from the start to the finish lay clear and arrow-straight along the beach. The chariot needed more room to allow the horses free movement, so Eumelos had chosen the inshore track, with the dunes to his left. A single runner needs no such space, however, so Achilles' path lay straight ahead of him along the crest of the beach, following the tideline just inland from the beached ships' sharp prows and the hawsers holding them, where the sand was further dampened by the spray blowing in from the surf.

***

As Nestor finally stood on the stony sand immediately between and in front of the combatants, a tense silence fell. The old king rode it for a moment, arms spread and level with his shoulders, heightening the tension as I sometimes did at dramatic points as I recited my epics. Then he dropped his hands to his sides and they were off.

Eumelos claimed my attention at once, leaning over the front of his chariot, shoulders hunched and arms spread, whipping the reins across his horses' rumps as he called them into action, not that they needed much prompting. They leapt forward, kicking up great sprays of sand seeming to go from standstill to full gallop in a heartbeat. The chariot rocked as it was jerked into motion, slewing towards the dunes, causing some of the onlookers there to leap back. But Eumelos' strength and expertise steadied things down at once and he was off, the wheels churning the sand into plumes behind him as he moved. All of this was so dramatic and arresting that I hardly paid any attention at all to Achilles who had leaped forward as swiftly as the horses and was pounding along the solid, stone-strengthened ridge of damp sand just inshore of the ships' hawsers and the stakes holding them. Or I didn't pay him any attention until the contestants reached the first stadion post and the observer there called, 'Achilles!'

By this time, I had seen Achilles do many things but I had never seen him run. Even back as far as I was, with less than perfect eyesight, I could see him quite clearly as he raced through the second stadion. His back straightened and his helmeted head came up. His arms, bent at the elbows, moved back and forth as though he was grasping the stormy wind so that it could pull him along. His legs pumped apparently tirelessly, hurling him further along that ridge of sand with every step. And the steps were amazingly rapid. Kicking up little clods of stony earth – but nothing to compare with the clouds and sprays generated by the chariot's horses and wheels.

The observer at the second stadion post called, 'Achilles!'

Achilles' head dipped, helmet plume flying, and for a moment I thought he had slipped. But no – he was simply, almost unbelievably, generating yet more speed.

The third observer bellowed, 'Achilles!'

The crowd, which had been cheering Eumelos on, began to fall silent, as though there was something magical, almost supernatural, here. The chariot still thundered forward, horses' hooves flashing, wheels spinning, carriage bouncing and leaping over ripples in the sand beside the dunes but still the fourth observer called, 'Achilles!' like all the rest so far.

The crowd, my family and my captain amongst them, flowed down onto the straight course as the contestants sped away. The further off they went, the more difficult it was to see which one held the lead, especially as the chariot seemed to appear and disappear behind the clouds of sand it was kicking up. The observers at every stadion post continued to bellow the name of their prince and general. Achilles sped relentlessly forward, all glittering gold.

Until, '*Achilles*!' came the distant call from the observer at the finish line. The word was hard enough to hear at that distance, especially over the bluster of the gale and the rumble of the surf but it was drowned out by cheering in any case, as even those who had lost wagers applauded a seemingly impossible victory. My father and brothers vanished into a crowd of men come to settle up. Nestor and Palamedes were no longer quite so happy to be leading them. 'You see how he did it?' asked Odysseus. 'How he strengthened his chances of winning while allowing Eumelos to do the exact opposite?'

'Even if the lad does, I don't,' said Diomedes. 'Why don't you explain it to me?'

I looked up in surprise, just in time to see the ghost of a wink and a smile in the Argive prince's expression. Diomedes's face was rounder than Odysseus' and clean shaven where the captain wore a full beard. The captain's hair was dark and flowing but his companion's was light and tightly curled. The eye that had winked at me was brown whereas Odysseus' was a strange greenish blue – aptly enough, a sea-colour. But there the differences stopped. Both

9

men were square, fit and strong with well-defined, athletic musculature. Both also carried an unanswerable air of command as easily as the cloaks that sat on their shoulders. Both were mighty warriors and able generals, Odysseus standing a little higher, perhaps, because he was a gifted captain and admiral. At least he would be an admiral as soon as he returned briefly to Ithaca and organised the fleet he was to lead across to Troy when the weather moderated and the wind changed.

iii

Diomedes had a reputation for kindness, and he was clearly happy to take some of the pressure off me for I still had no idea how Achilles had managed to ensure his victory. But, thanks to the Prince of Argos, I was about to find out.

I had seen Odysseus at work before and I knew that when he gave his explanation it would be based on observations that would seem childishly simple and I would almost certainly be kicking myself that I had missed so much that even someone blinder than I was could see with the merest glance. I looked up at Diomedes and saw that the Argive prince was frowning with concentration. Perhaps he too had been guided through the maze of one of Odysseus' explanations before – a maze that turned out to be a straight and simple path when you looked back at it.

'Let's start with Achilles' chosen course,' said my captain cheerfully. 'What can we observe from that?'

'It's the crest of a low ridge,' I observed.

'Good,' said Odysseus. 'And?'

'And yet it is flat and wide enough to allow ease of running...' said my companion. 'Though only just. There's room for a runner here but not for a chariot pulled by horses running four-abreast.'

'Well observed Diomedes. But that is just the beginning, surely?'

'The sand this close to the water is wet and solid,' I noted. 'Especially as there's spray blowing in from the surf.'

'It's full of stones too,' added the prince. 'Surely that must make it firm underfoot.'

'Yes! I said. 'We can see that because Achilles has left such shallow footprints,'

'Almost as though he was walking on tip-toe,' concluded Diomedes.

'Good! Well done both,' said Odysseus. 'So, even weighted with full armour, the runner had a track that was smooth and steady underfoot. One that actually aided his efforts to run fast and true. But what about his overconfident opponent?'

The three of us crossed towards the dunes. It was so obvious that the sand became dryer and softer with each step we took away from the tideline that it hardly seemed worth mentioning.

'Bearing in mind the tip-toe tracks Achilles left behind,' said Odysseus as he crouched beside Eumelus' starting point, 'the difference is clear. The wheels have not left tracks so much as trenches. The horses' hooves have left pits. Look at the way the sand has been scattered as the chariot slewed. It almost faltered here before Eumelus could get it back under control. That alone would have cost him the contest, but the situation does not improve. The chariot was by no means heavy, despite its trappings of gold and jewels, and yet it sinks into the soft sand.' Odysseus stepped into one of the wheel-marks. The sand on either side was level with his ankle. 'And for all their strength and power,' he continued, 'the horses found themselves fighting to move their hooves through the sand, let alone to pull the chariot behind them!' The captain glanced at me then turned to Diomedes. 'Not long ago,' he said, 'the lad here and I were bound for Skyros aboard my ship *Thalassa*. We were under oars and powering forward as swiftly as the ship would move. But we were sailing straight into a counter current so that every five stadions we moved forward, the current carried us back for four. Something similar has happened to Eumelus and his horses here. The damp stone-filled solid sand helped Achilles. But this...' he kicked the fine golden grains beside the wheel-marks, 'this fought Eumelus every stride of the way. He never really stood a chance.'

As if to emphasise Odysseus' words and prove the strength of his observations, the crowd parted and the chariot came thundering back. It approached much more slowly than it had departed, the horses cantering along the soft-sanded centre of the beach. It was being driven by its new owner, Achilles.

He reined to a stop and Patroclus took the lead horse by its head. The two young men said nothing but they exchanged enormous grins as Achilles pulled off his helmet.

\*\*\*

The air of mute celebration was disturbed by Prince Palamides of Euboea who strode past Odysseus as if the captain was invisible. 'A neat trick, Prince Achilles,' he sneered. 'So neat as to stink of double-dealing!'

He raised his right hand to point at the winner and I noticed that the golden arm-guards he had been wearing earlier were missing now.

'Did you make some secret arrangement with that grasping commoner with his tricky wagers? I have half a mind to...' His naked arm swung down as he reached towards his hip. But the sword he had been carrying there earlier was also missing now.

Everything froze for a moment. 'That's probably all that's keeping him alive,' said Odysseus quietly.

'What?' asked Diomedes.

'The fact that he wagered his sword and lost,' said Odysseus. 'If he'd actually drawn it, he'd have had to face Achilles blade to blade. No one's done that and survived so far.'

'I've got a good idea,' I said. 'I can go and ask my father to return it to him. Just until he and Achilles have completed their discussion.'

'An amusing notion,' said Odysseus. 'But let's allow the blowhard to live a little longer, shall we? Besides, I have a prior claim on him – he threatened the life of my son before he insulted your father and called Achilles' honour into question. I'm not sure which of those errors was the most dangerous, but mine certainly came first…'

But our whispered conversation was interrupted. 'Eumelus had every chance to choose his course and that was the one he chose,' said Achilles icily. 'If he hadn't been so overconfident he might well have won. It was a matter of tactics, not of boasting. Or of honour, as you call mine into question. If you want to discuss the situation further, I suggest you talk to him. If you wish to revisit the matter at any time within my hearing you had better bring a sword. And reserve your place with Hades in Tartarus first.'

Achilles stepped down out of his new chariot and turned his back on his accuser. Palamedes swung away in turn and strode off down the beach.

He was replaced by Nestor and the atmosphere lightened at once. 'You cunning young devil,' chucked the old king. 'I don't think I've seen such barefaced trickery since Jason fooled King Aeetes on his way into the store room where he kept his gold in Colchis. Swept princess Medea off her feet at the same time! Pretty little thing, but what a harridan she turned out to be…'

'Did you lose much, Majesty?' asked Achilles respectfully, clearly embarrassed at having caused the old man to have lost anything at all.

'Nothing I couldn't afford to lose. That's the secret of laying a good wager! Besides,' he turned to me and grinned. 'Your father will just take all the armour, weapons and so-forth he's won and swap them for some of Agamemnon's gold. Then when Agamemnon puts them on display, I'll find a way to get it all back again! Probably polished and sharpened into the bargain. By the way, Prince Achilles, I detailed a couple of your Myrmidons to help our rhapsode's family carry all their winnings back to Aulis. I hope that's all right – they were pretty well laden I can tell you.'

'So,' said Achilles, and the full weight of his dazzling gaze fell on me, 'You were so confident that I would win that you told your father to wager on it?'

'Yes, Majesty. But only because…'

'It was a remarkable show of faith in you, Achilles,' Odysseus interrupted me. 'I was most impressed by it. Perhaps we can persuade him to write a song about it and immortalise us all.'

Achilles' gaze narrowed, still resting on me like the weight of the midsummer sun. Then he grinned and became more dazzling still. 'We must discuss that, young rhapsode. Immortality, eh? And so easily won!' Then he turned away and it was as though the clouds overhead had grown a little thicker.

King Nestor's gaze moved onto Odysseus. 'Did Palamedes give you the message, Odysseus?'

'I'm afraid not,' said the captain. 'Palamedes was too busy talking with Prince Achilles to notice we were even here.'

'Hmmm,' said Nestor. 'Well, the messenger found us when we were with the lad's father and we promised to pass it on. There's a woman trying to find you and she managed to get to Agamemnon. He had no idea where you were so he's apparently sent her to your tent. She's probably there now, waiting to talk to you.'

iv

'You seem to have made a friend there,' said Odysseus as we walked back towards his tent. 'Achilles' favour is a precious thing. Not many men have won it. Patroclus has it, of course, though hardly any others do. I sit pretty high on the list at the moment, but only because I made it possible for

14

him to do what he wanted and bring his Myrmidons to Aulis – on the way to Troy and immortality, if he can snatch it from the gods.'

'You won his friendship for me, though, Captain,' I said.

'Perhaps I helped a little,' Odysseus admitted. 'But you aren't likely to thank me for that help unless the muses are co-operative in your poetic immortalisation of that epic contest.' He chuckled, then fell silent. I could see that he was preoccupied – and needed no great insight to realise that his thoughts had turned to the mysterious guest who was waiting in his tent.

The huge camp looked formless and haphazard, but there was in fact some order to it. The city of Aulis stood at its northern extreme, filling a valley that led down to the docks of our busy port, its main road running back up the valley and over the watershed to Thebes one complete stage or 160 stadia away. Aulis had served as Thebes' port in the days of Theban greatness. The days before the tragic reign of King Oedipus and his wife/mother Queen Jocasta, his fractious children and the catastrophic wars of 'Seven against Thebes'. The place was a ghost of its former glory now, but Aulis continued to flourish. The land running south from our city walls seemed simply to slope seawards, with the forested hills inland appearing to give way to a tilted plain sloping down to the shore. But that plain was not as flat as it looked. There was a hill at its centre rising a good deal higher than its surroundings. Unsurprisingly, Agamemnon, as High King, had pitched his sizeable accommodation here and, almost inevitably, the lesser kings had erected their quarters around it. Their various armies then spread out across the fields, in huge units centred round the command tents of their generals rather than those of their kings. And, where the king was also their general, then his most trusted lieutenant filled his place amongst his troops. Thus Achilles' tent was high on Agamemnon's hill and, as Achilles shared it with Patroclus, it was General Menesthios who camped with the Myrmidons.

The entrance to Odysseus' accommodation was guarded by two of his massive oarsmen who tended to swap their role for that of soldier when *Thalassa* was at anchor or – as now – beached. Their names were Eurylocus and Elpenor and I knew them well. I was struck, therefore, by their strangely formal stance. They knew they were usually there for show – Odysseus was neither rich enough nor unpopular enough to fear having his quarters rifled and the guards usually stood at their ease. Not now, however: they were at attention and as alert as if they guarded a fortune in golden armour.

'She's arrived, whoever she is,' said Odysseus quietly. He nodded to his crewmen, stooped and entered, pulling the heavy leather curtain of the doorway aside as he did so. Fascinated by the events at whose heart I suddenly found myself, I followed him without a second thought.

Odysseus' accommodation was practical but unpretentious – as befitted the man himself. An outer chamber, large enough for meetings and briefings, was lit by a couple of panels high on the leather walls which stood open now but which could be closed when the rain started. An archway covered by another curtain led into the captain's private quarters. A tall figure wearing a hooded cloak stood framed against this inner curtain, a shaft of dull grey daylight making her a thing compounded mostly of shadows, oddly colourless. I only knew her gender because King Nestor and my father had told me of it. The hood hid our visitor's face and the cloak concealed everything else.

'What does Karpathia, High Priestess of Artemis want with me?' asked Odysseus courteously.

*** 

The cloak parted. Two pale hands rose to push the hood back and I saw that whoever had described this woman to my father had not lied: she was indeed beautiful. Her face was long and pale, her nose perfectly straight, her eyes moss-green and shining with intelligence. Her hair was black and piled beneath the distinctive headdress of a High Priestess.

But it was not her beauty that struck me, it was her aura of power and authority. My first impression was that here stood someone as commanding as Penthesilea, the warrior queen of the Amazons, whose reputation nowadays was the equal of Hippolyta's, the Amazon queen who had captured even Theseus and made him her lover more than a generation earlier. But this was no warrior; her power was spiritual rather than physical. There was about her an air of unruffled calm which was only deepened when she spoke. 'How did you know me?' she asked.

'To begin with,' said Odysseus, 'there was your beauty.'

High Priestess Karpathia turned away frowning. 'Men have commented on that often enough. Usually with ulterior motives. I am not easily swayed by flattery.'

'You misunderstand me,' said Odysseus gently. 'Every report of your search for me has been accompanied by commentary about your beauty.' Karpathia began to interrupt, but he held up his hand, forestalling her. 'Reflect, High Priestess. Men could only comment upon your beauty if they had seen it. Which means that, despite the hood of your cloak, you have come amongst Agamemnon's army not only alone but without a veil. Very few women would do this. Some of the women whom my rhapsode's father is thinking of employing for the relief of the army, perhaps – but no such woman would be seeking me. A woman not only of beauty therefore, but a woman of power and sufficient standing to walk through an army unprotected, with her face bare. Other than those I have mentioned, such women are rare; unique, even.'

'Even so...'

'If I guess at a High Priestess, therefore, what shrine would she rule? Again, that is not too difficult a probability to winkle out. You presumably started your search for me in Aulis itself, for my rhapsode's father was first to mention you, and he, in his own words, *keeps his ear to the ground*. Which High priestess would have the power or the confidence to walk through the city before coming out among the tents? Why the High Priestess of the deity whose beneficence guarantees the safety and prosperity of the city. The High Priestess of the Temple of Artemis, therefore. Guardian of the oracle to whom High King Agamemnon has already made his approaches in the matter of this most unfortunate weather. Although I was not with him at the time, those who were have given me a precise description of the High Priestess, including not only her appearance but her name. So, Karpathia, High Priestess of Artemis, what is it that I can do to help you?'

The High Priestess studied Odysseus coolly, apparently utterly unimpressed by his logic. Then, 'They told me you were capable of unusual insights,' she said. 'And these relying on your own wits rather than on the help of the gods. I now see that the reports are true. Therefore I have a use for you and your logic, if you will exercise it on my behalf.'

'You have only to ask,' said Odysseus, but his tone reminded me of what he had said about Achilles and Agamemnon. He would work *with* the High Priestess – if they came to an agreement – but he would not work *for* her.

High Priestess Karpathia seemed to understand this as clearly as I did. 'The Goddess will be grateful,' she said. 'The matter is this. Some days since, just when the weather turned foul, the youngest and most impulsive of my priestesses vanished, seemingly without trace. You were right to suggest that my mission to find you began in Aulis. It began at the dwelling of her family, in case she had returned home for some reason. That was a faint, last hope, because we have been scouring the sacred groves and the woods nearest to them in search of her.'

'But she was not at home,' prompted Odysseus. 'And while you were seeking her there, some news reached you, making it more imperative that you find me.'

'You are correct,' said Karpathia. 'I had no sooner finished talking to her parents that word reached me. She has been found.'

'Dead, I assume,' said Odysseus.

'Murdered,' said the High Priestess.

## 2 - The Grove of Artemis

i

When I asked Odysseus later why he allowed me to accompany the High Priestess and himself, he said he wanted to make sure he would be immortalised alongside Achilles. But things had gone far beyond a joke by then. It was my belief that as well as his wife Queen Penelope he was missing his son Prince Telemachus and, although I had almost nothing in common with the infant prince of Ithaca, I somehow filled the gap left in Odysseus by his enforced separation from the boy. As I had observed to Father, I couldn't imagine anyone filling the void left by his separation from Queen Penelope. The depth of this loss not only underpinned his kindness to me but also his hatred of Palamedes who he blamed for the separation and for putting the young prince's life in danger in the cruel trick that unmasked his plan to avoid the war. But, whatever the reason, he did not stop me following him when he in turn followed the High Priestess of Artemis with Elpenor at his shoulder as she left Odysseus' tent and led us down the hill towards Aulis. As she did so, the priestess described what she had done on hearing the news of the missing girl's murder.

'I was beginning to fear the worst in any case,' she explained. 'Nephele was young and impulsive as well as beautiful – and only a couple of stadia away from fifty thousand bored and restless soldiers.'

As she said this, my father's description of Prince Aias came to mind – that he would rather rape a woman than romance her.

But the High Priestess continued talking over my brief flash of suspicion. 'When Nephele's family had no news of her I began to grow more certain that the Goddess must have taken the girl to herself. My only hope then was that the departure from this realm was swift and painless. I had just left the family's house when the messenger from the temple found me and gave me his terrible news. I saw the hand of the Goddess in this as well, for the messenger was only able to find me so easily because everyone at the temple knew I was going to see Nephele's parents. A few moments later and he'd have missed me. I would probably only have found out the truth when I got back to the temple myself and I doubt very much it would have occurred to me to seek your help then.'

'Did you go back and break the news to the poor girl's family?' asked Odysseus.

'No, I did not. I was too upset to consider it. The messenger's description of what my searchers have found made it immediately plain to me that I would need more than the usual guidance from the Goddess, though I am certain that it was She who put your name into my mind so swiftly. These are matters I can discuss with Pythia the oracle, who speaks directly to the Goddess herself from her sacred rooms in the temple. I told the messenger to return at once and order that nothing be touched or moved until I arrived to look into the matter. Then, instead of returning to the Nephele's family I came in search of you.'

'But you found Agamemnon instead.'

'That is not quite what happened. I have been in contact with the High King on more than one occasion in the recent past. His army has pitched its tents on land owned by the temple, and, as more and more divisions have arrived, the encroachment has worsened. I have had to discuss the matter of rent and terms of occupancy with him. But more important still is what he has discussed with me. Hardly surprisingly, the huge army he has been assembling here is not only encroaching onto land I am responsible for as High Priestess but it is also going through his supplies at a tremendous rate. He tells me he planned a short campaign, which is why he is calling together such an overwhelming force. But by trapping him here in Aulis the gods are undoing everything he had counted on. He has a war chest of course, but that is being squandered - as he sees it - on feeding and watering his idle troops instead of arming them and preparing them for immediate battle. Thus he has been sending out ever-larger hunting parties deeper and deeper into the forests in search of food that he does not have to pay for. Indeed, because he is as bored and frustrated as anyone else, he often leads them in person.'

'And they have further encroached onto ground that is sacred to Artemis, I assume.'

'They have. Though I am as well aware as anyone of the irony that the goddess of the hunt should forbid hunting in her sacred groves. But so she does, because she is also the protectress of wild things and wild places and there's an end to the matter.'

'Though that's not how the High King sees it?' asked Odysseus.

'Precisely. He is not a spiritual man. He is a pragmatist and is far more interested in worldly fame than he is in honouring the gods, so he sees the danger of angering them as much less important than the danger of running out of gold or facing the humiliation of watching his army deciding to go home and leave him stuck here alone. That is something he is beginning to view as an increasingly probable outcome unless he can find some way of changing the situation – or of persuading the gods to do so if he becomes sufficiently desperate to call on them. He is here in search of money and power – yet he discovers himself to be powerless in the face of the weather, wasting his gold at a rate he is beginning to find unacceptable and waiting for his army to walk away even before the final units have arrived. However, it is my duty to enforce the wishes of the Goddess, even in the face of his bluster. So we have had several conversations. In the temple, in the forest and in his tent.'

'So you knew how to find the High King and hoped that he

would know how to find me.'

'Indeed. When I explained the situation, he was unusually co-operative; probably relieved that the matter on this occasion did not involve him or his huntsmen.'

\*\*\*

This conversation took us down the hill, out of the camp, in through the southern gate and across to Aulis' central agora. Karpathia's chariot and driver together with two attendants were waiting for her here among the market stalls. The messenger who had brought the news about the murder had returned to the temple with her orders as she had explained. Karpathia questioned the attendants as Odysseus sent Elpenor to fetch his chariot and we waited for it to be readied, but they knew nothing more about the matter. 'It's probably just as well,' said Odysseus in the end. 'We don't want to be distracted by what other people saw, or thought they saw. We need to approach it with *fresh eyes*, so to speak.'

Like Achilles' recent acquisition, Odysseus' chariot was a light war-chariot, though pulled by two horses, and really designed for a charioteer and one passenger – a fully-armed hero who would be carried to the battlefront and leap down there challenging opponents to single-combat. In doing this the heroes gained not only glory but gold – the winner took the loser's armour, which was often gilded and bejewelled, as well as all his weapons. Elpenor took the reins, the captain stood at his shoulder and there was just room for me. Karpathia's chariot was a far grander affair, as befitted the High Priestess of the divine protectress of the city and its surrounding areas. There was plenty of room for her driver, herself and her attendants. As her chariot was also pulled by two horses, our speed out of the city on the road west toward Thebes was stately rather than urgent. Fortunately, the contest between Achilles and Eumelus had taken place early in the morning and it was only approaching noon as we left the city with the sun god Helios guiding his own blazing chariot to the apex of its daily course somewhere high above the heaving overcast.

Thebes may have been well past its fabled glory, but the road between it and Aulis was still busy, most of the traffic heading for the coast. The restless army trapped here attracted traders of all sorts and as I observed them hurrying hopefully like flies towards a honeypot, I wondered whether my father's father's father had once been just like them, or had he been more like Captain Odysseus, preferring to ply his trade aboard ship, giving even Jason and his Argonauts, perhaps, some stiff competition. Nowadays my father commanded almost as many vessels as wagons.

I was able to indulge in these dreamy speculations because the road west mounted a steepening slope which slowed the chariots' progress – something compounded by the traffic flowing against us like the counter-current that Odysseus had described which slowed *Thalassa* on our voyage to Skyros. Moreover, the distance between the chariots, the bustle of the traffic flowing against us and the constant bluster of the wind made conversation difficult. And once we got close to the heaving, roaring trees, impossible.

After some time, Karpathia's chariot turned left onto a broad track that was clearly both well-used and well-maintained. The noise of the wind in the trees became almost overwhelming and the dull grey light thickened further between the close-packed trunks of tall pine trees. The restless air, however, was fragrant with the scent of balsam. The track led up through the trees to the holy precinct. This was a wide area that had been cleared of trees, levelled and flagged by earlier generations of workmen and worshipers. Behind this space, the hillside rose in two sheer steps, each one taller than several men but level at their tops as far as I could tell at this distance. At the centre of the lower space stood the temple. It was lined on all sides with columns that supported the main roof but within these stood the solid walls of the building itself. Three great steps reached up on all sides from the precinct to the outer columns then two more stepped up to the inner walls. A processional stairway started well back from the main entrance and led directly up to the doorway in the inner wall. The High Priestess' chariot drew to a halt by the foot of these stairs and Elpenor guided Odysseus' chariot to a standstill beside it. 'I must cleanse myself and consult the oracle,' she said. 'The temple servants will guide you to a place where you can rest and refresh yourselves then we will follow those who found poor Nephele to wherever she is lying.'

Male temple servants came out to take our horses and chariots to the stables while others led us into the temple itself where female servants and junior priestesses led us further in. The temple was designed similarly to the royal halls I had seen at Phthia and Skyros. There was an entrance area that led into a reception area with a huge, square formal megaron further in still where four columns stood in a square around the circular pit which contained the sacred fire. There was further accommodation deeper behind the megaron but we did not get a close look at it. Instead, we were led to one side of the reception area where there was seating and some low tables adjacent to it. Bowls of water were brought for us to rinse our hands and faces. Linen cloths arrived for us to dry ourselves. There was more water to drink and wine to mix with it if we wanted. There was bread, oil, olives, honey and cheese so that by the time the High Priestess returned, we were clean, satisfied and ready to follow her into the sacred groves of Artemis which had been so brutally desecrated.

ii

At first I assumed that it was the nature of our mission which made High Priestess Karpathia so grim and thoughtful as she led us back out of the temple, following the two servants who had discovered the murdered girl. But suddenly she started talking to the captain and I discovered she needed to share a burden that she found heavy and, as it turned out, dangerous.

'Pythia the Oracle was very specific,' she said. 'The Goddess has dictated that whoever did this must pay for it, like for like. Until the debt is settled, Agamemnon and his army are going nowhere – unless they choose to go home. But even if they do that, they will simply be postponing the inevitable. Somewhere, sometime, the debt must be paid, like for like. Pythia says the Goddess has told her that a member of Agamemnon's army is involved. I must see the High King once more and tell him to seek out this man – or all his plans and hopes will come to nothing. I pray that you can help me discover sufficient information to make the High King's task quick and easy.'

I paid scant attention to the last few sentences spoken. The repetition of the phrase 'like for like' distracted me, made me think of my father's wagering earlier that day. On the beach beside the race course the phrase had precise meaning. Prince Palamedes had wagered his gilded arm guards and his jewel-hilted sword. If Achilles had lost, my father would have given him another pair of arm guards and another sword – gilded and bejewelled, like for like. The race had gone the other way, so Palamedes had lost his arm guards and his sword. It looked as though whoever was responsible for the young priestess' death would have to lose a child of his own in exchange. Or he would have to do so if Pythia the oracle was really in contact with the Goddess, and that was truly what Artemis had demanded. The thought made my blood run cold – *what if whoever did this dreadful thing was working for Father? Could my life possibly be forfeit?*

The path from the precinct into the forest was lined with cypress trees, and the resinous scent they gave off was heady but their dark green foliage seemed to make the day darker still and as the wind gusted through them I fancied that they were singing a sad song. A dirge, perhaps, for the poor dead girl. The two searchers led us unerringly through the undergrowth. The woods around us grew wilder. I imagined that there would be snufflings, stirrings, birdsong and sounds of movement had the wind not been so loud in the trees. Instead, there were flashes of movement up in the branches and out amongst the tree-trunks with the low bushes that grew sparsely between them. I found these confusing as the effort of keeping up seemed to make the flashes of brightness at the edges of my damaged vision more vivid. As we proceeded, the going got harder because the hillside we were walking across was folded into ridges that grew higher and valleys that grew deeper. It was still possible to make progress, however, because the undulations were not too extreme at first, though as I limped onwards I started considering whether I should break off a sturdy branch to use as a crutch.

But my disabilities did not blind me to what was going on around me. Odysseus' gaze was everywhere. Walking beside him, I could make out the tilt of his head, the angle of his face and the movement of his eyes. He glanced up above our heads every now and then; looked from one side to another for longer periods, but most of his attention was focussed straight ahead, on the ground beneath our feet. I too tended to look down, for the combination of pine needles, fir cones and sparse grass made our way quite slippery because the last day or two, since the arrival of the stormy weather, had been wet. Beyond that, I had no interest in what was going on beneath my feet. Or rather, I didn't until, seeing where I was looking, Odysseus said, 'Yes. Hoofprints. There have been horses here.'

The High Priestess heard him, though he was speaking to me. 'Horses,' she echoed. 'And horses can only mean one thing. Hunters. As the oracle said.'

'Are these amongst your sacred areas?'

'We are about to enter the grove of the Goddess. The area and every plant and animal within it is sacred.'

'And, most sacred of all, I assume, will be the deer.'

'Deer are more than sacred to the Goddess. She has been known to transform herself into a deer on occasion. The virgins of the temple tend the deer of this forest and have as an act of particular holiness gilded the antlers of the great stag who is king over them all.'

The conversation ceased after that but we did not walk in silence for long. Our guides slowed as they led us to the crest of the next undulation and stopped there, standing back as we approached. Where the ridge-crests so far had given onto downward slopes, this ridge ended in a low cliff. Even I could see that the ground and the vegetation along the cliff-edge had been violently disturbed. The earth was churned, with the footprints of people and animals intermixed. The bushes had been torn and broken; some of them were hanging over the edge of the low precipice, dangling by their roots.

'Watch where you're treading,' ordered Odysseus as he walked towards the edge. Obediently keeping an eye on our feet and the ground beneath them, we followed him. The little cliff of mud and stone was about three times as tall as Elpenor the better part of two kalami high, but this was only obvious with careful observation for there were more bushes growing at its foot that reached between a third and half-way up it. Like the bushes at the top, these were battered and broken, some of them obviously dying. Other than that, I saw nothing but Odysseus said, to Karpathia, 'Yes. I see her. Someone has moved those dead bushes to cover the body. Could you ask one of our guides to go down and remove them, carefully, please?'

The High Priestess gave the order. One of her servants scrambled down and pulled the bushes aside. And there was the dead girl, lying face down in the mud and rubble, her head at a strange angle, one arm clearly broken and the stub of something covered in blood sticking up out of a huge russet stain on the left side of her back.

\*\*\*

'Where to begin...' said Odysseus softly to himself, 'where

to begin…' He stood where he was, like the rest of us looking down at the corpse a couple of kalami below our toe-tips. Then he looked up. 'I assume your searchers are adept at tracking – that would be why you chose them to come looking.'

'Of course. Ikaros there has been a hunter in his time but now he serves the Goddess and protects the lives of her wild subjects. That's why he's the leader of my search parties.' She gestured to the searcher who had not scrambled down to move the bushes but who stood beside us at the moment, looking sadly down at the corpse. This was a scrawny, hunched man of advancing years, who nevertheless shared with King Nestor, a lively athleticism and a sharp gaze that suggested an equally sharp mind. 'Ikaros,' said Odysseus, 'I see the tracks of at least one horse here. The footsteps of a man approaching from the undergrowth back there, perhaps leading the horse. I see more footprints coming out of the bushes behind you, those of a woman or youth walking on tip-toe, or, more likely, running. And there is something else here I can't quite make out…'

'I'm surprised you can see that much, Captain,' replied the retired huntsman. 'These pine needles are near-impossible to track through. But yes: footprints – two sets as you say. Round, solid hoofprints. But I don't think you mentioned seeing these.' Ikaros pointed to the ground nearer the edge of the little cliff. 'More prints near the same size as the hoof prints, but these are split, do you see? Split prints. There was a sizeable deer here.'

'Ah, yes. I see its tracks now coming out from the bushes there, approaching this point and then, nothing.'

'Where did it go, then?' asked the High Priestess, her voice demonstrating her further concern that whatever had happened here had not only resulted in the death of the girl but in some sort of danger to a sacred animal.

Odysseus and Ikaros exchanged a glance, then Odysseus said, 'It went over the edge.'

'You mean it jumped? I've heard that stags will make some astonishing leaps but this one would need to be the Goddess in disguise, surely…'

'It didn't leap,' said Odysseus. 'It fell. And Nephele fell with it.'

'But why?' demanded the High Priestess. 'How could such a thing have happened?'

'That's what we're here to find out,' said Odysseus. 'Let's go down for a closer look.'

Ikaros led the way. His companion who had moved the bushes had found a fairly easy path on his way down to do so and we all managed to get down without any mishap – even me. We walked along the foot of the little cliff until we had reached the dead bushes and the dead girl they had covered. Looking up from here I was struck by the unexpected height of the cliff and how sheer it appeared to be from this angle.

I had expected Odysseus to approach the corpse at once but yet again he did not meet my expectations. Instead, he turned and began to look more closely at the dead bushes. 'These have been crushed by some considerable weight,' he observed, then he looked around, turned his back on the cliff altogether and examined the ground once more. The pine needles were disturbed by a wide track, as though something heavy had been dragged through them. 'There's something strange here,' he said. 'Ikaros, can you follow those tracks? Don't go too far but stop and alert us if you discover anything that strikes you as odd.' The trees were not so tight-packed down here and the bushes between them were sparse. Even so, Ikaros vanished amongst them in a moment.

At last Odysseus turned to the corpse. 'Eyes first and most,' he said. 'Hands next and least. What can we see on and about our poor subject just as she is before we move her for a closer personal investigation?'

'Her neck and arm are broken,' said the High Priestess, the slight unsteadiness in her voice the result of outrage, I suspected, rather than shock or horror.

'Just so. Most of her ribs as well, judging from the shape of her chest and the way whatever has pierced her is standing so far out of her back. I should observe also that there is a most unusual amount of blood staining her tunic, even allowing for the terrible damage done to her body. Like the bushes, she has been crushed by something heavy. Probably at the same time as the bushes were squashed and by the same weight falling from the same place.' Odysseus pulled the bushes further aside and approached the body, his gaze, strangely – at least strangely to me – seemingly looking everywhere except at the subject of his investigation. This approach almost immediately bore fruit. The cliff above the dead girl's oddly-angled head seemed to have been scraped by a set of claws, as though a gigantic eagle, had attacked it. Odysseus' attention focused on this and he followed it downwards, until, with a grunt, he reached into the mud and pulled something free. He held it up so that we could all see it. At first I thought it was a tooth almost the length of his thumb or the tusk of a wild boar, for it came to a point like the fang of a massive wolf. But then he rubbed it, clearing away the caked mud. As he did so, he explained, 'It's a piece of an antler.'

As the mud came off, even in the dull and shaded light, we could see a gleam of gold.

iii

Elpenor and Ikaros' companion helped Odysseus and me pull the dead bushes further back still. The captain stepped right up to the body's side and went down on one knee in the mud. The young priestess was wearing the clothing associated with her goddess – the chiton tunic ending at her knees which was designed to give the goddess freedom of movement when she went on the hunt herself. It was belted at the waist, something we could only see because her cloak was bunched against the face of the mud-cliff, except for the part of it anchored by the stub of wood which stood above that massive puddle of dry blood. Nephele wore no rings nor any jewellery that we could see. Her sandals were unusually solid – but that was, no doubt, to allow the priestesses to move through the wild places sacred to their special deity. I glanced at the High Priestess' sandals – they were equally robust. I looked back just in time to see Odysseus reach out and touch the dead girl's tunic just above her hip, testing the edge of that great bloodstain. 'Damp,' he said. 'She's clearly been here since the weather changed – not that there's been a huge amount of rain, just the overcast and the storm wind.' He leaned back, never taking his eyes off her. 'I think we need to turn her over now,' he said. 'But, High Priestess, if I am going to help you and the High King unmask whoever did this, I am going to have to look beneath her clothing at some point.'

'I had expected that to be the case,' said the High Priestess matter-of-factly. 'Some servants from the temple will be here soon with a litter to carry Nephele back there. Once certain rituals have been observed, you will have the chance to examine her more closely.'

'As long as the rituals do not include washing her before I have examined her,' said Odysseus.

'I will consult the oracle,' said the High Priestess.

'Very well,' said Odysseus. 'We need to turn her over now.'

The four of us took gentle hold of the poor girl's corpse and rolled it towards Odysseus, away from the foot of the cliff. It seemed to me that the body moved strangely, though I had not dealt with many corpses. 'Because so many bones are broken,' said Odysseus when I mentioned my impression. But his tone was pensive, his attention clearly not on me and my observations. I fell quiet, therefore, and did my best to apply some of the suggestions he had made earlier. *Eyes first and most...* The dead girl's face was dark; in fact the front of her body seemed somehow duskier than the back. Her shins seemed darker than her calves; her toes darker than her heels – but not arrestingly so. Nevertheless, her wide eyes and gaping mouth, both at a strange angle like her face and head, were disturbing to look at so I focussed my attention elsewhere. The foot of the cliff we had uncovered was not a precise angle, such as the bottom of the temple walls made with the flagstones on which it was built. Rather it was rounded; seeming to suggest that when Nephele fell she started a small landslide. Beyond the edge of this, the ground was dry, apart from a circle of deep brown where the mud had been given an autumnal hue by the poor girl's blood. This was echoed on her tunic itself, because the entire front of the garment was covered in dust and pine-needles which slid off when we moved her. Only that red circle seemed to cling to these things, turning the dry dust to sticky sludge. The red circle was centred towards the inner slope of Nephele's left breast as far as I could judge but there was something about it that disturbed me. I couldn't work out quite what this was until Odysseus observed, 'There's nothing there.' And I realised I had unconsciously looking for the flights of what I assumed to be an arrow, for I couldn't imagine what else the stub of wood sticking out of her back could be.

'How could that be?' I wondered.

'Either it snapped off as she fell, like the point seems to have done, or it was driven further in when she landed. Or, I suppose, it might have been pulled further through by whoever or whatever snapped the shaft sticking out of her back. Whatever happened seems to have drained her of blood at a great rate. I have seen corpses on the battlefield a day or two after death who are white on the upside but black on the downside. It can only be the way the blood settles. But we are getting ahead of ourselves…'

Whatever the captain was going to say next was interrupted by the return of Ikaros. 'I think you ought to see this, Captain,' said the old hunter.

Odysseus continued to stare at the corpse for a few more heartbeats then he turned. 'Very well, Ikaros. What have you found?

\*\*\*

It didn't really need the skills of a hunter to follow the trail that started beside the corpse and the dead bushes. Whatever had made it – presumably the stag whose gilded horn Odysseus had just found – must have been severely injured itself, not least by the uncharacteristically clumsy tumble off the cliff. But just because the trail was easy to follow did not mean that we should pay no attention to it. For instance, it seemed that there were footprints right at the very edge of it, heading one way and then another, but these were almost impossible to see and only Ikaros commented on them with any confidence. And then a stadion or so from the cliff, Ikaros paused and pointed to something a little more obvious.

'I see,' said Odysseus. 'A man leading a horse joins the track here. Presumably the hunter from the top of the cliff. He follows the deer deeper into the forest. But he doesn't come back this way - not with the horse, at least - does he Ikaros?'

'No, Captain. That's part of what I have to show you.'

'Very well,' said the High Priestess. 'Lead on then.'

Ikaros led Captain Odysseus, the High Priestess, myself and Elpenor even deeper into the forest. 'These are the most sacred groves of all,' said Karpathia quietly. 'Reports abound of men and women seeing the Goddess herself here; sometimes in her own shape with her huntresses and hounds in attendance, sometimes in the shape of a deer. Pythia the oracle has even suggested that it was in these woods, not on Mount Kithaeron that the hunter Actaeon discovered the Goddess bathing – so she turned him into a stag and had his hunting dogs tear him to pieces as he tried to run away.'

'I see,' said Odysseus carefully. 'It is clearly a very dangerous thing to get on the wrong side of Artemis.'

'It is dangerous even to call her by name in these woods,'

warned the High Priestess.

'I'll bear that in mind,' said Odysseus.

'Here we are,' announced Ikaros.

We had just entered a clearing. It was disturbingly circular in nature as though drawn by some great mathematician - or formed by some deity. At its centre stood the tallest cypress tree I had ever seen. Ikaros led us straight to it and stopped. 'This is the heart of the sacred groves,' said Karpathia quietly. 'This is the sacred cypress. The Goddess inhabits every element of it. We need to be very careful what we do and say here; very careful indeed.'

'But the deer came here,' said Ikaros. 'And so did the hunter.' He stood looking expectantly at the captain. Odysseus stood, eyes busy, forehead folded in a frown of concentration. 'The deer made it to the tree,' he said slowly. 'That much is clear. And the hunter with his horse followed it.' He fell silent, then squatted, observing the ground at the base of the tree-trunk. 'And this is where the deer died.' Suddenly he stood up and strode perhaps ten podes away from the rest of us. 'Blood spatters here,' he observed. 'Stretching further away still. It was clearly crippled, but it wasn't dead so he cut its throat and let it bleed. I've seen horses killed that way after being hurt in battle and the blood can spurt up to thirty podes with astonishing force.'

Still frowning, he walked back to the tree. This time he looked up. There was a solid branch sticking out perhaps ten podes above the ground – one and a half times Elpenor's height. 'When it was dead, he slung a rope up there, you can see where it has damaged the bark; the branch is bleeding balsam. So he obviously lashed one end of it to the deer's hind legs and pulled it up off the ground. He must be very experienced and well-equipped, and have his horse well-trained, because he was able to make it stand still here while he lowered the carcase onto its back, retrieved the rope and led his laden horse away. The hoofprints going this way are much more pronounced than the ones we looked at earlier.'

As he spoke, so he followed the hoofprints, no doubt seeing the hunter and his laden horse in his imagination. But then, right at the edge of the strange circle, he stopped.

'The horse stopped there,' said Ikaros. 'I couldn't work out why…'

'Maybe he needed to adjust the carcase,' I suggested.

'He needed to do something to the carcase,' said Odysseus, looking all around himself. Then suddenly he swooped, like an eagle diving on a lamb, thrust his hand into a nearby bush and straightened. In his fist was the barbed head of a long hunting arrow.

iv

The temple servants who brought the litter had also brought a sheet of linen to cover its passenger. They appeared almost immediately after we had returned to the site of the murder – the *first* murder, insisted the High Priestess in whose eyes cutting the deer's throat ranked as high as killing the girl. As Artemis' earthly representative in Aulis, she felt this especially because the act was done at the foot of the Goddess' most sacred tree – to which her sacred animal had no doubt pulled itself seeking celestial aid. She shared every obol of Artemis' divine outrage as she made clear on the walk back from the sacred tree to the dead priestess.

'So,' said Odysseus almost to himself as the litter was making its careful way down from the clifftop, 'what can the site of the crime tell us before we and the victim must leave it?'

'Surely the site has told us everything it can,' I said. 'The corpse must tell us her story next…'

'No,' said Odysseus. 'There is more here.' He stared at the young woman fixedly, his mind clearly racing. As he did so, the bluster of the wind increased, finally reaching us down here and blowing a little cloud of dust from the dead priestess' clothing. As it did so, a large drop of rain found its way through the roaring branches and fell on the dead breast, just beside the hole in her tunic which no longer quite covered the wound made by that part of the arrow still in her chest. 'Of course!' he said. 'The dust!'

'What do you mean?' asked Karpathia.

'Her back was damp – it had been made wet by the rain that arrived with these storm clouds. But her front is dry. The ground beneath her is dry, except for the area soaked by her life-blood. The storms must have arrived almost immediately after she and the deer were killed!'

'That will be the rage of the Goddess,' said the High Priestess. 'It's all just as Pythia the oracle predicted. And there will be more to come until this matter is resolved and the blood-debt paid.'

At this point I had another flash of insight like the sudden realisation that if Father had been the man who did this, then my own life would be in danger - like for like. And my moment of revelation was about Father and his business once again. For it suddenly seemed to me that unless and until the Goddess was satisfied then his ships would be every bit as trapped here as Agamemnon's. Indeed, he could well find himself in the High King's situation, seeing his stores of wealth and provender vanishing while he had no way to replace them. It was in that moment, I suppose, that I stopped being a mere observer and decided I had better start playing a more active part in the investigation alongside my Captain – to the best of my ability at least.

In the heady grip of this new determination, I followed the litter back to the temple, walking at Odysseus' left shoulder while the High Priestess walked at his right. There was nothing new for us to observe, or discuss, it seemed – for we all walked in silence. We arrived at the temple steps and went up until we were level with the first raised section but still outside the columns. Karpathia went in to consult the oracle because – in spite of her wide experience and the decisive confidence it brought – she had never faced a situation like this before and was concerned that if she allowed the body to enter the temple itself she might be guilty of some kind of desecration. And, as we were becoming equally convinced, if the Goddess actually existed and wielded divine power, she was a very dangerous being to get on the wrong side of.

So we waited outside the temple as the rain which had warned us of its approach with that one great drop finally arrived. Odysseus frowned with frustration. 'Elpenor,' he commanded, 'help me move the litter into some shelter.' Elpenor obeyed without hesitation and I too stepped forward to help while the temple servants stood aghast at the apparent sacrilege. But no sooner had we moved the litter out of the downpour than the High Priestess returned. 'The Goddess is content for us to bring Nephele into the temple and to examine her there,' she said. 'There is no need for special ceremonial at this stage. The body will be washed and prepared in the cold room below the temple in due course.'

'The Goddess is content that we examine the girl down to her naked skin?' Odysseus said, his tone questioning.

'Down to the skin,' agreed the High Priestess, 'if it will speed the process of finding the murderer and avenging his crimes.'

***

First of all we moved one of the tables in the outer chamber into the strongest light. Then the servants carrying the litter held it steady while we lifted the corpse and moved it onto the table. It lay face down, as it had on the litter, because of the arrow-shaft sticking out of its back. Odysseus lifted the linen cloth clear but told the attendants to keep it handy. There was the dead girl's modesty to be considered when we did get down to her skin. Once she was on the table, the captain gently straightened her broken neck so her head was no longer at that disturbing angle then he did the same for her arm. He looked down at her, lost in thought. I did the same but I saw nothing of any importance. If my eyes were idle, my nose was working – the body was emitting a stale smell. So were my ears; it seemed that I could hear furtive movements of tiny creatures that I could not see.

'Right,' said the captain after a few moments. 'Let us begin.'

Working slowly and methodically, calling on my help and Elpenor's as he needed, the captain first removed the cloak, sliding the pierced cloth up off the clotted shaft, folding it and putting it aside. This revealed the entirety of the huge stain on the girl's tunic which had been partially covered before. He paused pensively, starting down at it.

'You observed that she had lost a lot of blood, Captain,' I said quietly.

'I did, lad. But I don't think this is all hers.' As he spoke, he brushed away several ants busily foraging the edges of the stiffened circle. 'It is obvious that the deer landed on top of her after they fell together. Its blood has been added to her own, clearly; and that explains the excessive quantity we observe.'

While we had been dealing with the cloak and discussing the quantity of blood on her tunic, the High Priestess silently gestured for the temple servants to remove her sandals. So, as soon as the back of the tunic was revealed, we were in a position to start removing it and once Odysseus had completed his examination of the blood-stain and given the footwear a cursory glance, we began to do so.

I was by no means old in those days but I was unusually experienced for my age. In various ports and cities which I had visited in my voyages aboard my father's trading vessels, I had seen athletic competitions of all sorts, from the leaping of bulls in Minos to competitions of running, wrestling, jumping and throwing stone balls, javelins and discoi. I had also attended gymnasia in many places, both to exercise myself and to observe athletes going through their paces. These had been performed by young men and women equally – all of them either partially clothed or naked. True, I was just of an age to consider courtship and marriage, but that part of my life had been frustrated by the damage that had been done to my face and body on the docks at Troy. However, the simple fact was that the unclothed female form held neither secrets nor any great allure for me. So I was able, I believed, to view the dead girl simply as a kind of challenge appealing to my intellect rather than to any other part of me, even as we removed one layer of her clothing after another.

In any case, as we rolled the body from side to side, lifted, laid and eased her tunic up past her waist, her modesty was protected by a simple undergarment which had become somewhat soiled and went a long way to explaining the odour hanging around the body, just as various insects, ants and spiders scuttling out of folds in her clothing and flesh explained the whisper of sound I believed I had heard. In order to ease her tunic over the stub of the arrow we had to roll her over and sit her up. I took hold of her head, being the nearest to it, and held it as steady as I could until Odysseus eased the garment over it and laid it aside. As well as the undergarment around her loins, she was wearing a strophium bound round her chest just beneath her breasts. The cloth band was loose because the chest around which it had originally been wrapped was much flatter now. There was a large, ragged, blood-rimmed hole in the front of this that matched the much smaller wound in the back from which the arrow-shaft was still protruding. 'We need to pull this out,' said Odysseus. 'Is it likely that the Goddess will mind?' He asked the question in all seriousness. The request was a courtesy at the very least. I had never discussed his belief in the gods with him but I supposed him to be sceptical rather than anything else. He was after all, a man who liked the kind of proof you could see, touch or arrive at through logical reasoning rather than by blind credence. Even so, the atmosphere in the temple and the absolute conviction of the High Priestess and everyone else nearby had a disturbing effect.

'No,' said Karpathia. 'Proceed. We would have had to take care of it at some stage of the cleansing rituals and preparation for her funeral rites in any case.'

V

By the time the High Priestess had finished speaking Odysseus had taken hold of the arrow and done his best to pull it free – but he found he was unable to do so. 'Elpenor,' he said at last. 'I had supposed it would be easy enough to pull this out, as many of the bones nearest to it are broken, but I was wrong. You're far stronger than me – stronger than anyone I know except for Prince Ajax.'

The massive warrior took the shaft surprisingly gently in his huge fist and, while the captain and I held her in the sitting position, he used the massive strength he had acquired as an oarsman to pull the arrow right out. I had expected a sucking sound followed by an issue of some sort of liquid. Neither of these things happened. The binding beneath her breast, however, slipped down to her waist now that there was nothing holding it in place. At last we could lie her on her back. After I had placed her head in a steady position, I took the linen sheet and folded it over her waist while Odysseus examined the arrow Elpenor had handed to him. He had brought the head end which he'd discovered in the bushes and the two pieces fitted together perfectly.

'But you see,' he said, as though speaking to himself, 'the break is not square. The shaft has split along the grain leaving two sharp ends. That would surely only have been done if the arrow was being pulled and twisted until it broke. We know it was pulled or pushed because that is the only way in which the flights could have penetrated the poor woman's chest. But, as Elpenor and I have already demonstrated, the power needed to accomplish this is considerable. We further know that the force needed to break the shaft in this way must have been even more considerable than I first suspected, because the flights and the head prove that this was an arrow of the highest quality, such as kings, princes, generals and only the richest could afford. The sort of arrow I have seen men risk their lives to scavenge on the battlefield. And the head is barbed – a proper hunting arrow; recognisable to a certain circle of men perhaps – hence the pause at the edge of the grove of the Goddess to cut it free and discard it'

'But,' I said, 'surely that would be wasted effort, Captain, because whoever is responsible for this was going to bring back to one part of the camp or another, a stag with golden antlers. Never mind the arrow – who is ever going to forget that?'

Odysseus gave a weary grin. 'Well reasoned, lad. So, at some stage or other we will have to return to these woods in search of a pair of golden antlers which have been cut free and hidden.'

'But in the meantime, what have you actually discovered?' wondered the High Priestess.

'We have discovered precisely what happened I think,' answered Odysseus. 'And it is this. A lone huntsman, well equipped, with a well-trained horse, came to your woods on the afternoon before the storms started. He was hunting deer and ended up tracking your stag. We know he was alone – otherwise the precautions he took such as hiding the body and discarding the arrow would have been a waste of time and effort. I have already explained how we know he was well equipped and riding a well-trained horse. He tracked the stag to the top of the cliff and shot it there. But the moment he loosed his arrow your fearless young priestess here leaped out from behind a bush where she had been hiding unsuspected, and threw herself in front of the holy animal. The huntsman's arrow – fired from an extraordinarily powerful bow – went through the girl's chest and deep into the stag's side. The wounded animal and the dying girl went over the cliff together, linked by the shaft of the arrow. The stag's antlers caught in the cliff-face so that when it landed the girl was underneath it. Its weight squashed her and drove the arrow deeper into the animal. In its pain and panic it pulled itself up, forcing the arrow flights deep into the dead girl's chest before the arrow-shaft finally split apart. Then it dragged itself to the foot of the great cypress you say is most holy to the Goddess. The huntsman came down from the top of the cliff, saw there was nothing to be done for the girl and covered her with the crushed bushes, then he went after the stag and did to it all the things I described in the clearing from slitting its throat to pausing and cutting the arrowhead free. And that, apart from the fact he must have hidden the golden antlers somewhere and probably got soaked as the storm broke on his way home, is that.'

***

'The High Priestess seemed pleased,' I said as Elpenor guided the captain's chariot back towards Aulis through the rain. 'Which is not surprising. Not only can she prepare her heroic young priestess for her funeral now, but you have also told her everything about the man who murdered Nephele except his name. You certainly narrowed things down; there can't be all that many hunters so richly and excellently equipped. And if we can find more arrows like that one we'll have narrowed things even further...'

'And if we come across a tent that has a pair of golden antlers decorating it, we'll have done better still,' he teased. 'I don't think you've quite grasped how many men in Agamemnon's army might fit into that description. I can think of twenty kings and princes without actually exercising my mind. And beneath them there are their generals and assorted commanders. Take Achilles as we've spent a bit of time with him today. With Achilles you have Patroclus of course, then you have the generals of the various Myrmidon divisions: Menesthisos, Euodoros, Peisander, Phoenix and Alcimedon. That's seven in all – all equally excellent hunters, all equally well equipped, I'd say; all equally keen to keep their men well fed. Multiply the twenty kings and princes I've just mentioned by Achilles' seven associates and you have one hundred and forty suspects before you even start looking at the problem closely!'

I refused to be downhearted. 'But Artemis must be as pleased as her High Priestess,' I said. 'Surely, if we keep a careful look-out we will see the hand of the Goddess guiding and helping us.'

'I find that the gods help those who work hardest at helping themselves,' he said.

'Well, we certainly do that, Captain,' I said. 'Further, the Goddess has to be put into a better mood by the fact that the High Priestess will have completed the rituals of cleansing and finished the rites of funeral very soon. Then we can be certain that the Goddess has welcomed her priestess to herself.'

We fell silent then and Elpenor urged the horses into a faster trot. The rain eased almost immediately, and by the time we reached the city's western gate, the clouds were beginning to depart – in a straight line stretching across the sky from the northern horizon to the southern horizon. It was as though Helios the sun god was wearing the thick overcast as a cloak and pulling it away after him as he guided his golden chariot down into the west. The sky over the bay and the island beyond it was clear, calm and blue.

'There,' said Elpenor. 'That looks as though you've satisfied the Goddess after all, Captain.'

Odysseus grunted, unconvinced, but I thought the massive oarsman was probably right. I went to bed content that night, therefore, looking forward to the coming dawn with some excitement.

But when I got up next morning, I found myself at the centre of a dead calm under a blazing sun in an atmosphere so thick and heavy that I found it hard to breathe.

The Goddess, if she existed, was clearly not satisfied after all. Quite the opposite, in fact.

## 3 - The Hand of the Goddess

i

There were those who saw the hand of the Goddess in the way that matters worsened so swiftly from such a promising beginning. At first, it looked as though the change in the weather was positive and yet Agamemnon's mood and those of his highest commanders remained dark and unpredictable setting a tone that soon spread through their armies like a plague. With little else to do, the High King and his closest advisors began to revisit their plans for the voyage that they expected to be undertaking as soon as the wind returned to blow from a more favourable quarter. They also began to review their decisions as to how best to divide the loot they would get from the sack of Troy, seeking to strike a balance between those who supplied the greatest number of warriors, those who added most to the war-chest and those likely to be the most important in battle. This confronted them with the names of the kings and princes who had yet to fulfil their promises to send ships or soldiers or both; a lack of commitment the volatile Agamemnon began to interpret as a direct attack on his standing and authority.

Furthermore, the restless leaders soon began to suspect that the oppressive calm was destined to last as it sometimes did at this season, and a dead calm was no more helpful to their plans than the storms it had replaced, for it was too hot to row the warships for any distance – and towing the fat, square-sailed, wind-reliant freighters full of their horses, equipment and supplies was simply out of the question. As time went on, Kalkhas the army's soothsayer, was summoned peremptorily and consulted repeatedly. But he only gave one worrying prognostication after another.

Right from the beginning it seemed to me, as someone born and raised in Aulis, that we were stuck here, helpless, until the next new moon at least, whether this was the work of the Goddess or not. All that had really changed was that we had traded a constant chilly drizzle on the wings of an easterly gale for windless, burning days and sweltering nights. We had moved from too much water to nowhere near enough. My own situation also underwent an unexpected and nearly fatal change. The main reason for this was that the High King suddenly insisted Odysseus should return to Ithaka at once and complete his organisation of the Cephallenian fleet he had promised to bring from those islands off the western coast, of which Ithaka was the most important.

I sensed something sinister in the atmosphere on that first morning almost immediately after I woke. I had spent the night sleeping aboard the beached *Thalassa* as we arrived back at camp too late for me to get past the guards on the gates into Aulis and my chances of going home were therefore non-existent. The city fathers, Father amongst them, had instituted a curfew and closed the gates at sunset soon after the first lethal confrontation between outraged citizens and drunken soldiers on the hunt for amenable companionship; preferably, but by no means exclusively, female. High Priestess Karpathia was not the only local dignitary who had enjoyed increasingly discordant face-to-face negotiations with High King Agamemnon. And the result of these negotiations was that the gates were locked and guarded every evening. They were hardly comparable with the great gates of Troy, but they were quite sufficient to keep all the soldiers, their kings and commanders, firmly outside the city.

I had just climbed down onto the sand at dawn on that first windless morning, therefore, and was standing assessing the change in the weather when King Nestor came hurrying up, his face folded into an unaccustomed frown. 'Is your captain aboard, lad? I'm looking for him.'

'No, Majesty,' I replied. 'Have you tried his tent?'

'Yes. He's not there. Have you any ideas? High King

Agamemnon wants to see him.'

'No, Majesty. May I help you search for him?'

'Yes. I want to ask you something anyway.'

\*\*\*

We set off side by side and I had to hurry to keep up with the sprightly monarch. Unlike more pompous kings and princes such as Prince Palamedes of Euboea and Prince Aias of Locris, Nestor did not stand on his dignity – if he saw a task that needed doing, he was in action. Where a lot of the others seemed to delegate everything to soldiers, slaves and servants, Nestor just got on with it himself, even though as the High King's most trusted advisor he was effectively in the top rank of commanders, and one of the few that senior whose army was sharp and well-trained. This was because it was in the hands of his sons the Princes Antilochus and Thrasimedes. The other young generals, Achilles and Diomedes, were the same, always in action and regularly training alongside their troops. Odysseus was also always in action of course, though his troops had yet to arrive. Unlike my captain, however, Nestor made no allowances for my damaged limbs and eyes. 'What's this I hear about Odysseus getting mixed up in the murder of a priestess from the Temple of Artemis?' he demanded as we rushed through the encampment.

'The High Priestess Karpathia asked him to look into the matter,' I answered. 'She was the mysterious beauty you told us had been looking for him yesterday.'

'Yes. I see. Well, it's all over the camp. What did he discover?'

I told him everything about the previous day's adventures, my sentences getting shorter and eventually broken as I ran out of breath, weakened by the speed we were moving at and the increasingly sultry atmosphere we were hurrying through.

'So, he's certain the girl was killed by one of our hunters?' demanded Nestor when I arrived at my last gasp.

'At the moment he shot the sacred deer, yes, Majesty,' I wheezed. 'And the killing of the deer has apparently upset the Goddess almost as much as the death of her priestess.'

'So,' continued Nestor after a moment, 'this High Priestess, this Karpathia, has convinced Odysseus that Artemis is taking personal revenge on the whole army because of this, and will not relent until the guilty man admits his sin and sacrifices one of his own children in recompense?'

'That's what the High Priestess and Pythia her Oracle believe. I am less certain about what the captain believes.'

'Nevertheless, the High Priestess wants Odysseus to help her unmask this culprit and so appease the angry goddess?'

'Even though he does not actually believe that the Goddess Artemis is really causing anything that is going on now or is likely to happen in the future. Yes.'

'Hmmm. Of course, for once it may well turn out to be irrelevant what Odysseus believes. It is, however, crucial what Agamemnon thinks and decides. And, beyond that, even, what the army thinks. *And,* in my experience, the situation will not be helped by this change in the weather.'

'How so, Majesty?'

'It promises so much, presents such a welcome change, and still it will do more harm than good unless it changes again soon. I remember when I was with Captain Jason on the *Argo* we had a spell of weather like this. At first we thought *fine,* there's no wind but the sun's up and the sky's blue – we'll just furl the sail, break out the oars and row. But rowing under a sun like this is hard work, even when Hercules is helping, and we were soon parched. Then we realised how little drinking water we had aboard. That's why we went ashore in Mysia, just up the coast from Troy; a fatal mistake as it turned out. Hercules' young companion Hylas found a spring of clean water leading down to a sizeable lake, then the simple-minded boy managed to drown himself in it. We found him floating face-down wrapped in pondweed. There was some talk of naiads tempting him in too deep but it looked like a stupid accident to me. Hercules left the ship as a direct consequence and by Zeus we could have done with him later…'

'So, surely, Majesty,' I ventured, fearing that this was the beginning of another of the old king's endless reminiscences, 'the High King will want Odysseus to do what the High Priestess wants.' I gasped a breath but managed to proceed before he could answer. 'The faster the guilty man is unmasked and the blood debt settled, the better,' I said, with absolutely no idea of how naive I must have sounded to the elderly politician.

ii

I began to discover my failure to understand the workings of power almost immediately. Odysseus was still not in his tent so I followed Nestor on up the hill to Agamemnon's more palatial accommodation as the old king gave me a set of instructions about what I was to do if Odysseus wasn't in the High King's tent either. All of which came to nothing, because he was there after all. I couldn't see him but I recognised his voice which I could hear though the leather walls. 'Off you go, lad,' said Nestor as he walked past the guards at the entrance. 'I hear him inside.'

I turned obediently away, but the conversation from inside the tent – which was quiet but intense – caught my attention. So I went to the first unguarded section of that leather wall, squatted there, and started to pay proper attention to what I could hear while pretending to take my ease and try to catch my breath, prepared to lie that I had no idea I was so close to the command tent if challenged.

'Back to Ithaka? *Now*?' Odysseus snapped. There was very little respect in his tone.

'Kalkhas predicts that this weather will likely last, and some of the local seafarers agree, so he says. Not that he needed consult them. He has lived on both shores of our sea – born and raised in Troy before he emigrated to Achaea;

because he foresaw my attack on the city and the great victory it will bring. Apollo revealed it all to him, so he says. Victory and riches to us, ruin and destruction to his birthplace, so he was wise to move out if what he says the God predicts is true. In any case, we're still stuck here and not going anywhere for a while longer. It's a perfect opportunity! Are you telling me you can't do it?'

'Of course I can do it, Agamemnon! Even in this weather!'

'Good! Because it's starting to give a bad impression if one of my senior lieutenants hasn't managed to organise his fleet or his army yet, especially amongst the commanders and their troops who are stuck here day after day!'

'I can leave *Thalassa* beached where she is and get across to the west coast on horseback or by chariot!' snapped Odysseus with unaccustomed vexation. 'It won't take long to organise the fleet – it's only a dozen ships after all. Then if it looks as though a slow voyage back is in prospect I can come ashore and return by horse or chariot. My Cephallenian fleet has enough competent captains to do without me on the voyage round here to Aulis. But it means I'll be away for ten nights, maybe longer.'

'In the unlikely event that we've left by the time you return, you and your Cephallenians can catch up. You know where we'll be headed!'

'And the situation the High Priestess of Artemis has asked me to look into?' grated Odysseus. 'What about that?'

'Give the details to Prince Palamedes,' ordered Agamemnon dismissively. 'He'll take over. Besides, I have a further mission for you if you're going by road. King Tisamenus of Thebes still hasn't arrived with the army he promised me and he can make it in spite of the weather. He just has to march - where everyone else has to sail; and it's not a very long march either! You did such a good job tracking down Achilles, perhaps you can give him a nudge as well.'

'Palamedes. You'd send Palamedes into the Temple of

Artemis? *Palamedes*?'

'He doesn't have to go anywhere near the Temple of Artemis. He has to find the name of the man who hunted that god-cursed deer and accidentally killed that stupid little bitch who, you now inform me, actually threw herself into the path of the arrow on purpose. So in spite of what the High Priestess and her Oracle seem to think, it's not a case of murder at all. It's self-slaughter. This Nephele creature clearly had some kind of wish to join her goddess at the earliest possible moment and the hunter – whoever he was – just helped her fulfil it!'

'It's more than thirty stages there and back,' said Odysseus sometime later. He was talking to Elpenor back at his tent but I was close by as usual. One stage was equal to 160 stadia; that would make it 80 leagues each way. A considerable overland journey followed by a short voyage; no wonder he thought it would take at least ten days. 'But we only need to pack for five nights or so; we can restock when we get home. I don't want to overload the chariot or slow us down with pack-animals. Half a dozen competent riders as escort should do – you pick them and see they're well provisioned and very well armed. We'll leave Eurylocus in command of *Thalassa* while we're away. He's level headed and reliable if unimaginative, which is probably a good thing too. We're going via Thebes on the road west to boot King Tisamanus into action; better do that *after* he's given us a bed for the night. We can stop at Onchestus, Cyparissus and Crisa as well, they're all a day or so's journey apart along our route. Then we can take a ship either from Chalcis or Calydon. Thank the gods he didn't want us taking messages to his Queen Clytemnestra in Mycenae on the way!'

\*\*\*

'But why, Captain? Why send you away now?' I asked later still as he oversaw the final preparations for his departure. 'He knows you haven't organised your fleet earlier because he sent you and King Nestor searching for

Prince Achilles! He knows that! And it's only eleven ships other than *Thalassa*. He's got more than a thousand out in the bay already…'

Odysseus looked at me with an expression I recognised – I had seen my father use it when I or one of my brothers said something embarrassingly naive. 'I suspect that in the final analysis his decision has been motivated by Nephele's death and the Goddess' reaction to it,' he explained patiently. 'The outcome of any investigation has the potential to be disturbing and quite possibly destructive both to the army's morale and the High King's authority. Especially as he has the better part of fifty complete armies sitting here, bored, restless and on the lookout for trouble. Would he really dare order one of his royal generals to bring one of their children here as a blood sacrifice in recompense for a dead priestess and a sacred stag as Karpathia and Pythia say the Goddess demands? No. Such a demand would probably start a civil war *here* at Aulis when he wants to fight *Troy*. So whoever is found to have done this must either be someone of no account, someone with no children or someone who is not associated with the army and preferably never was. He doesn't trust me to make sure the investigation goes the way he wants it to, so he's sending me away and handing it over to someone who will discover exactly what the High King wants him to discover!'

'But isn't that a bit short-sighted, Captain?' I wondered, shocked at the barefaced dishonesty of it. 'Prince Palamedes' investigation won't satisfy the High Priestess unless it discovers the truth. Unless the right man is unmasked and the right child sacrificed, it won't appease the Goddess either.'

'No, it won't. So let us hope that the Goddess is actually far less interested in the actions of we puny mortals than the High Priestess and her Oracle would have us believe!'

And that was that – or so I thought.

In spite of the fact that he was unhappy at the thought of leaving Palamedes in charge of his investigation, Odysseus was clearly excited at the prospect of seeing Queen Penelope and young prince Telemachus again, even if it would only be for a short while. The route west he was proposing was the logical one – though to be fair there was another that branched to the south at Thebes and ran down through Corinth if he had actually wanted to take a message to Agamemnon's court in Mycenae for any reason. Messengers had been coming and going between the High King and his Queen on a regular basis ever since we arrived. Odysseus wasn't by any means the only husband and father missing his beloved wife and children.

Later still, Odysseus turned from his final conferences with Prince Palamedes in his bivouac beside his Euboean army and acting captain Eurylocus on board *Thalassa* and caught sight of me still lingering at his tent. 'Ah,' he said. 'There you are. I've been thinking about our earlier conversation and I have a mission for you.'

A shiver seemed to go down my spine at his words and the hair on my good arm stirred.

'I assume you thought you'd be able to stay at your father's house in the city with your feet up, eating your mother's cooking and growing fat while I was away...'

'I had thought I would stay aboard *Thalassa* and compose some epic songs in your absence, Captain...' I did not manage to sound wounded by his jocular accusation, I was too excited by what he had just said about having a mission for me.

'Hmmm. Well, I have asked King Diomedes to keep an eye on you instead. Neither has a rhapsode with them. He will often be in attendance on Agamemnon for one reason or another. I want you with him at every possible opportunity. I have asked him to give me a detailed report when I get back on what Agamemnon's plans are as near as he can discover them. But from you in particular I want to know what Prince Palamedes has been up to. I don't trust him and I don't like the fact that he's been put in charge of finding out who killed the priestess and the sacred deer.'

'So,' I said, 'you *are* concerned about the Goddess and whether she really needs to be satisfied after all!'

'As I'm sure your father has pointed out sometime in your over-active youth, you can never be too careful.'

'A sentiment I rather wish I had borne in mind that night on the docks at Troy,' I said ruefully.

'But even that experience, dreadful though it was, might betray the hand of the Goddess,' he observed gently. 'If you had been more careful that night in Troy, you would not be here now – and then who would I be able to trust to keep a secret eye on things at the heart of power during my absence?'

iii

Sometime earlier in our acquaintance, Odysseus and I had a discussion about murderers. I expressed surprise when he suggested that the most successful murderer will be someone who does not even remotely appear to be a murderer. Anyone who is obviously a murderer is unlikely to get away with it for long, if at all, he maintained. I told him that I could hardly believe that the Gods would possibly allow such a creature to exist, and he said they manifestly do, indeed they take the lead in the matter of disguise. Zeus himself, for reasons of desire rather than murder, appears in the shape of a swan, of a bull, of a shower of gold, hiding his true nature from the people he wishes to deceive. It is by no means beyond mortal ingenuity to imitate the gods. Events soon after we had this conversation proved Odysseus' observations to be true as he unmasked a murderer who did not appear to be in the slightest like a murderer.

I was already beginning to discover that his observations were also true in the matter of spying; the most efficient gatherer of intelligence was someone who did not appear to be doing so at all; in fact someone that hardly anyone even noticed.

One afternoon some days after Odysseus had departed for Ithaka, King Diomedes came and found me on *Thalassa* where I had taken up residence. 'Agamemnon is holding a feast tonight,' he said. 'But it appears that he has sent his rhapsode away to carry a message to his wife. Nestor suggested that you would be a good replacement; he says your epic songs are particularly entertaining.'

'Possibly because they are about people he knew in his youth and occasionally feature him alongside them, Majesty,' I observed. But I was flattered that he had made the recommendation. Or I was until I realised that Odysseus had almost certainly asked him to do so as part of the plan we had discussed. This was a realisation driven home by Diomedes at once. 'Remember,' he said. 'You are not only Odysseus' rhapsode; you are his eyes and ears. You will have access to places Agamemnon would hesitate to let either myself or Nestor into; you will hear conversations he would never hold in front of us. He doesn't fully trust either Odysseus or Odysseus' friends.'

'But a rhapsode, of course, is of no account and easily overlooked,' I said. 'Little more than a piece of the furniture.'

'You must have been talking to Palamedes or his crony Aias,' he chuckled. 'That's just the way they see their soldiers, slaves and servants!'

I spent the rest of the day practising and perfecting the epic song I proposed to perform. It was an old favourite, the first that Odysseus had ever heard me sing. One that was particularly apt for this occasion as it dealt with an earlier attack on Troy by Hercules and his piratical gang of heroes. It was also one which Nestor knew so well that he must – I prayed – have already told every story it reminded him of. Then I changed my chiton for a clean garment and put a formal himation over it, took up the leather bag in which I carried my lyre and went up the hill as the sun sank westwards on my left shoulder and the watch fires, lamps and candles were ignited like earthly stars all across the camp and the distant city in the purple-shadowed valley beyond it.

There was no wind, of course, but as I neared the High King's tent I smelt the odour of roasting meat. *Thalassa*'s crew and I subsisted on a diet of coarse barley bread, olive oil and fish. At first the scent was so overpowering and sweet that I could think of nothing but my salivating mouth and rumbling stomach but as I came nearer so my head began to clear. The army's main meat supply – certainly for kings, princes and generals – was a combination of mutton and goat liberally mixed with a range of fish and fowl. Some had been brought in the various armies' supply trains but the vast majority of it had been traded with Father and his local colleagues; the shepherds, goat herds, fowlers and fishermen of Aulis. But, dim though my eyes might be on occasion, my ears and nose seemed sharper in compensation. And a very few more breaths made me realise that what I could smell was neither kid, lamb, goat or mutton. It was venison. And venison could only have come from the wooded hills behind the city, where the Groves of Artemis stood.

\*\*\*

High King Agamemnon's tent was a smaller, leather-walled, linen-lined version of his citadel in Mycenae, which I had not seen but knew to be similar to those I had visited in Phthia and Skyros, if reputedly more magnificent. It was also, I realised, disturbingly similar to the Temple of Artemis. The formally guarded entrance led into an ante-room where visitors could divest themselves of cloaks and so-forth if the weather was cold or wet. Here they could also be requested to deposit any weapons they might be carrying. But the guests tonight appeared to be Agamemnon's most trusted allies, so there were no swords or daggers to be seen out here. Next, there was a reception area where guests could mingle informally, drink and hold social conversations. Further in still was the big, square, formal megaron, already set out to feast the High King and his guests. Four great columns supported the pinnacle of the tent's roof and stood around the great circular fire beside which the festive victuals were being ceremonially prepared. Beyond and behind the megaron were the domestic sections which, in the palace at Mycenae would house Queen Clytemnestra and the children, Agamemnon's son and heir Prince Orestes and his beloved daughters the Princesses Electra, Chrysothemis and Iphigenia. Here, the area was much smaller, of course – just enough to house the High King, his staff, his personal servants and his slaves.

Hardly surprisingly, I was lost amongst the kings and princes who thronged the reception area, but King Diomedes had been looking out for me. He took me through and put me into the keeping of Oikonomos, the High King's chief steward, who in turn showed me where my place at table would be and where my stool would be positioned when I was called upon to perform. Beyond that, there was nothing for me to do. I could not possibly sit before the guests were assembled, in their places, until Kalkhas had said the ceremonial prayers to the gods and the High King had directed us to be seated.

It looked as though the main section of the dinner was going to be the venison I had smelt on my approach, whose odour now filled the megaron like a miasma. There were birds of various sorts roasting at the fire beside it and what looked like a large fish – perhaps a shark. But this was basic battlefield fare, even though it fed kings. There were olives, cheese and flat breads made of white wheat flour on the tables but the venison would clearly be the backbone of the meal.

The tables were arranged around the walls, with a throne at the centre of the high table for the High King to sit in, then the boards ran across one side and down the two at right-angles to it. There was seating for perhaps twenty, counting myself. As I tuned my lyre and rehearsed my song silently in my head, I amused myself by trying to work out who would be seated where. But before I had come to any conclusions,

Agamemnon led his guests through from the reception area and I saw for myself who went where. Agamemnon in the central throne, of course. His brother Menelaus, the jilted and cuckolded King of Sparta sat at his right shoulder with Prince Palamedes of Euobaea, on his. Aias of Locris close beside his friend and neighbour, Locris and Euobaea being parted only by the narrow bay running north between Aulis and Phthia. Then came the King of Athens Menestheus, Elphenor King of the Abantes, Leonteus of Argissa and a couple more I did not recognise. On Agamemnon's left sat King Nestor of Pylos, the oldest man present, with King Diomedes of Argos, among the youngest, beside him; then Agapenor of Arcadia, Idomeneus of Crete, the massive Ajax of Salamis, golden Achilles Prince of Phthia, and of course Patroklos beside him, almost as close in their association as Palamedes and Aias. The end of one line was brought up by the soothsayer Kalkhas who would perform the priestly rituals and the other by the physician Machaon. And finally, of course, me.

The feast proceeded in the formal manner favoured by the High King who wished to emphasise his importance and authority over restless generals and a fractious army. I studied the leader of this vast undertaking as the choicest cuts of all the creatures roasting by the fire were carved from the carcases, piled on a great platter and carried to Agamemnon first. He was a square man of middle height and middle years. Others here were taller, stronger, better-looking, younger, more virile, older and wiser. But there was about Agamemnon a sense of power that was so great it hardly needed to be expressed or emphasised. He was in many ways, it seemed to me on this my first chance to study him at length, like the great lion that his hair and beard made him so much resemble. His heavy-lidded eyes were golden. His straight nose flared into broad nostrils and his lips were straight and thin, tending to turn down rather than up at their ends. It seemed simply inevitable that the steward and his assistants should carry that great, smoking platter to him first above all.

To the High King of all Achaea who, as was his royal right, made his selection, which Oikonomos sliced off for him, with a few regal gestures.

After Agamemnon was satisfied, the pile of steaming meat was separated onto two lesser platters. One was offered to Menelaus, his elder but lesser brother; and the other to Nestor. So the diminishing piles of food moved step by step down the ranks of those present until at last an all-but empty platter arrived in front of me. All that was left upon it was a charred and unappetising-looking shank which was bent into a hook-shape. But it was venison and I was hungry so I took it. I laid it on the flat bread which was there for the purpose. Had it been larger, I would have taken out my cheap, wooden-handled dagger and cut pieces off it as most of the other guests were doing. But it wasn't really big enough to warrant it. So I picked it up as I would have picked up a chicken leg and bit straight into it.

iv

The meat beneath the black and bitter crust was sweet. I tore off a sizeable mouthful and began to chew. But almost at once a disorientating sensation swept over me. My mouth was full of something that tasted unmistakeably of venison but the venison seemed to be full of sharp bones just like a mouthful of fish. With a certain degree of caution, I eased the largest of these to the front of my mouth and pulled it past my lips. It was a long shard of white bone, much more substantial that even the largest fishbone I had ever encountered. Several other sharp white fragments joined it before I dared swallow. I looked at the shank more carefully, twisting it so that I could see clearly past the tendons to the shaft of bone my first mouthful had uncovered. It was completely shattered. I looked beyond my almost inedible meal to the carcase by the fire. Even stripped of most of its flesh and all of its limbs, it was still a strikingly large animal. One that, sometime during its death and journey here, had managed to break its foreleg so badly that its bone had completely shattered. One animal that might have suffered such an injury sprang immediately to mind – the deer which had crushed Nephele as they fell to the foot of that cliff together.

Deep in thought, I separated the meat from the shattered bone with the utmost care and consumed it slowly, sending a quick apologetic prayer to the Goddess in case I was eating her alter-ego and begging her to forgive the sacrilege if so. As I did this, I revisited in memory that wide track which stretched from the foot of the mud cliff to the cypress at the heart of the sacred grove. It was indeed just such a track as a lame creature might make as it dragged itself along on broken legs. The more I considered the matter, the more the certainty grew on me that we were eating the very deer whose death had started all this; even including the unnatural weather if the High Priestess and her Oracle were right. As chance would have it, if I was careful I might get an opportunity to test my growing certainty, for I was the only person at the feast other than Oikonomos and his cooks who would be going close enough to the fire to examine the remains. This was the kind of freedom, I thought, that Odysseus wanted me to make full use of. The inconsequential, unconsidered and apparently insignificant spy.

Obviously any deer, large or small, being served at Agamemnon's feast would have been killed or wounded by arrows and may well have sustained a broken leg at some stage of its journey from the forest to the fire, but this particular deer would surely have further damage not unlike Nephele's. Hers, for instance, might not be the only broken ribs just as hers were not the only broken limbs. I completed my meal of venison, wrapped the broken bone in the flatbread as though the bread were a linen cloth, and slipped it into the bag containing my lyre. Odysseus might find it interesting to see it when he returned, especially if I could prove it did in fact belong to the animal involved in

Nephele's death and perhaps even discover who had killed them both. For someone, sometime during the last few days, must have presented the carcase to Oikonomos for gutting, skinning, hanging and preparing for the feast.

Then, as Kalkhas led the blessings and Agamemnon began the formal round of toasts, I thought through what the shattered bone seemed to reveal, what else I should look for when I got the chance to approach the fire and the carcase beside it, and how I thought Odysseus would proceed in the matter if only he were here and how he would wish me to proceed now that he was not. I was so deep in thought that Oikonomos had to call me twice before I realised it was my time to perform. I opened my bag again, retrieved my lyre, rose and walked towards the fire. What was left of the deer was spitted there, stripped to the bone. This was just the condition that was most useful to me, for I saw with a calculatedly casual glance that several ribs had in fact been damaged. I would only be able to discover the precise detail of the damage with longer and closer examination but this was a good start. I decided that my absent captain would almost certainly try and get a closer look at it as soon as possible; and I would need to find a way to do that myself, therefore.

Then I drove all such thoughts from my mind, crossed to where the rhapsode's stool had been placed and sat. I wedged the lyre into the club of my left arm and closed my left fist firmly on it, closing my eyes in apparent sympathy as I allowed my song to fill my mind. I struck the strings with the fingers and thumb of my right hand and sang the epic of my own composition, following Hercules in my memory and with my words on his fatal path from the Trojan docks toward the Citadel, the Palace and the doomed King Laomedon, King Priam's father. The song retold the tale of how the notoriously parsimonious King Laomedon made the fatal mistake of trying to trick Hercules by breaking his word and reneging on a deal he had sworn to fulfil after the Hero rid the kingdom of a terrible lion. In his rage, the cheated Hercules killed the old man on the spot – and so King Priam succeeded to the Trojan throne. It wasn't quite the same as stealing the King of Sparta's wife, the High King of Mycenae's sister-in-law, the woman who many of the most powerful men in Achaea had sworn to protect at any cost, but it was close enough:

*'Sing, Muses, of the anger of Hercules, black and murderous, costing the Trojans terrible sorrow, casting King Laomedon into Hades' dark realm leaving his royal corpse for the dogs and the ravens. Begin with the bargain between the old king and Godlike Hercules. Strong promises the old king broke calling forth the rage of the son of Zeus...'*

\*\*\*

'An inspired choice,' said King Diomedes. 'If you ever get tired of traipsing around after Odysseus, there's a nice comfortable place for you at my court in Argos.'

'Agamemnon was extremely pleased with it,' emphasised Nestor, joining Diomedes beside me as the feast began to break up. 'I'm sure he'll want to hear more of your songs. Well done!'

I gaped at him at a loss for words. I had been sufficiently pleased by the fact that he had not interrupted my performance with one of his stories this time.

'You seem to know the back-streets of Troy suspiciously well,' added a cold, sneering voice. 'It makes one wonder....'

I looked up to see Palamedes standing close by with the shorter, slighter figure of Aias of Locris at his side.

'... about spies and double agents and so-forth.' Aias finished his companion's sentence, echoing his unpleasant tone.

'If you're worried about people who know Troy too well,' snapped Nestor, 'then I suggest you have a word with Kalkhas. He was born and raised there!'

The pair of them turned away together and as they did so, Oikonomos appeared. 'The High King wishes me to inform you that he very much enjoyed your song,' said the steward. 'He had commanded that I give you this as a token of his appreciation.' As he said this, he handed over a silver handled dagger in a jewelled scabbard. 'The High King looks forward to hearing more of your songs.'

'Thank you,' I said, a little overcome. 'Please thank the High King for me. I will be honoured to perform my songs for him at any time…'

Oikonomos nodded companionably and turned to go, but I recovered my wits quickly enough to call him back. 'Excuse me, Oikonomos, but do you happen to know which hunter brought in the deer we have just been eating?'

He turned and looked at me, eyebrows raised. I had to admit it was an unusual question. But I had no sooner asked it that I realised both Nestor and Diomedes were also focused on the answer the steward was about to give because they both knew precisely why I had made the enquiry in the first place. The steward's gaze moved from one of us to the other, the faintest of frowns wrinkling his brow. 'Why yes,' he said. 'That carcase was brought in several days ago – just as the storms started. It has been prepared and hanging in preparation for tonight's feast.'

'And which hunter brought it in?' prompted Diomedes.

'Not one hunter but two,' answered the steward. 'Prince Palamedes and Prince Aias brought it in together.'

'Two of them,' said Diomedes as the steward walked away. 'That complicates matters. I wonder which one of them killed it? As I understand matters, that will be the man the Goddess is after.'

'What's the matter, lad?' asked Nestor. 'You look surprised.'

'I am, Your Majesty,' I replied. 'I was with King Odysseus when he went over the ground with Ikaros, the man who found the body – a hunter who had become a servant of Artemis. And at no time did either of them say that there had been two men involved. One set of footprints; one set of hoofprints. I followed them myself. It was one man...'

'What does that mean?' wondered Nestor.

'At first glance,' said Diomedes, 'either Odysseus and this tracker Ikaros got it wrong, and there were two men involved in the death of the priestess and the sacred stag – and if I had to suspect anyone it would be those two. Or Palamedes and Aias killed an entirely different deer and that's what we've been eating tonight.'

'But if that's the case,' said Nestor, 'then where is this sacred stag?'

'And if that's the case,' I echoed, 'it's surely quite a coincidence that another dead stag turned up just as the weather turned bad. Because that's what betrays the hand of the Goddess. That's what has got us all stuck here. That's what got King Odysseus involved in the first place...'

'Is there any way we can check further, I wonder?' said Diomedes.

'Only one way I can think of at this point, Majesty,' I answered.

v

The huge camp settled to sleep. The lights went out as lamps and candles were snuffed. The embers of the watch-fires glowed or guttered. The still air was as clear as spring water, though still heavy and hot. The sky was huge and packed with stars all clustered round a fat moon a few days past full which was on the rise behind the spiky ramparts of the forested hills where Artemis reigned supreme. I paused on the cool sand beneath *Thalassa*'s forepeak and looked up at them, wondering superstitiously whether the Goddess was there herself tonight. I hardly needed the lamp I had taken along with my new dagger and the arrow-head Odysseus had left aboard in the belief that the ship was safer than his tent, all packed in a stout leather bag – except for the lamp which I carried carefully though it was as yet unlit; I didn't want to lose all the oil before I found what I needed its bright flame to examine. I crept out of *Thalassa*'s shadow pretty well-laden therefore as I started on my secret mission but if I was going to spend any time in close examination of my objective, I would have been foolish to rely on moonshine. And creeping through the camp right up to the edge of the forest, I would have been foolish to rely on my old, wooden-handled weapon when this gaudier but deadlier alternative had come into my possession.

Spending time on *Thalassa* rather than in my family home brought me to a new understanding of the fundamental practicalities of life in a camp this size. *Thalassa*'s crew performed their ablutions and dumped their rubbish over the stern which still sat in shallow water swept by currents strong enough to carry the effluent away. The beach was also trenched with carefully maintained latrines that were scoured clean with each high tide. Further inland, there were cesspits. But as though the entire army was one great living thing, it produced other waste products that required disposal in places other than the sea. Each contingent of every army had a midden heap where camp waste was piled – everything from rags of uniform gone well beyond mending to the bones and offal of animals and fish consumed at feasts such as the one I had just attended. These stood like a series of hillocks in the empty zone between the upper edge of the encampment and the lower fringes of the forest. These tips were piled high and noted for their stench, especially now that the sun was heating up the days. A little more fearsome sunlight and they would start to burn – either spontaneously or lit by tidy-minded soldiers who didn't want their nostrils offended any further. It was a simple enough matter to work out which of these piles contained the waste from Agamemnon's tents. It did not require the logical reasoning of my captain to be certain that the carcase of the deer would be one of the most recent additions to it. I just hoped that the heap would not be too high and that the bones I wanted to examine were not right up at the top if it was. It never really occurred to me to worry about what else might be interested in the rubbish, which showed how much I had yet to learn about life in the sprawling camp – and the life in the forest that crept out at night to feed on its refuse.

This ignorance simply arose from the facts that I had spent the recent nights either in my family home in Aulis or aboard the beached *Thalassa*. I had not slept in a tent out here. As soon as I moved away from the grumbling surf-line, the stillness of the windless night was broken at first only by the snoring, mumbling and muttering of thousands of sleeping men. There were no guards posted and no security patrols. We were, after all, nowhere near enemy territory as yet. However, despite the fact that I was surrounded not by one army but by many, I suddenly started to feel alone and lonely. As I moved along the makeshift pathways up the hill towards the High King's tent, so nature began to establish itself. Cicadas sang more loudly, it seemed, with every footstep I took. Then there were snufflings and the occasional howl of wild cats singing to the moon. Half-wild dogs panted and growled but ran away as I approached them. As it had been with the deer when it was cooking, all I had to do was follow my nose from Agamemnon's tent and it led me to the refuse dump, though this time the odour was anything but appetising, especially as it intensified with each step I took towards it. Worryingly, both my nose and my ears also began to warn me that there were other, larger, animals foraging the pile of waste matter. This was a moment of mild revelation, for I had not considered the matter properly. My own song came back to haunt me – for there were lions this side of our sea that were just as big as the lion Hercules killed for king Laomedon of Troy; though to be fair they were few and far-between these days. There were, however, bears, almost as sacred to the Goddess as her beloved deer. There were, as the scar on Odysseus' leg attested, huge wild boars.

The rubbish pile was at the centre of a clear area up-hill from the camp and close to the undergrowth that spilled out of the forest in low, dark waves. The restless movement of the scavengers interspersed with the occasional grunt, snap or snarl together with the intensity of the stench explained its careful isolation well enough. Although the moon was high now and bathing everything in a cold silver light, I paused, pulled out flint and steel and lit my lamp, gripped by an unnerving suspicion that I was being watched, and not by a friendly Goddess.

*\*\**

The circle of golden brightness cast by the steady flame in the still air was enough to disturb the nearby animals and I held it high, peering into the darkness all around until I was satisfied that there was nothing large enough to hurt me nearby and that the feeling I was being spied upon was a simple case of nerves. Then, turning back to the pile of rubbish, I focused the lustre of my lamp-flame on the nearest slopes. I managed to find the remains of the stag without too much trouble and approach it without having to climb the rotting hillside on which it lay. As the Fates would have it, the ribs I needed to examine were uppermost. The ribs reached out in a rounded shape like the struts supporting the sides of *Thalassa*, but the ones I was most interested in did not follow exactly the same curve as their closest companions: instead of bowing out, they bowed inwards. Moreover, my closer inspection showed quite clearly that the two ribs lying close together at the centre of this slight indentation each had a groove or nick in their opposing edges. These two marks were immediately opposite each-other. I didn't need Odysseus to tell me what they were. I transferred the lamp to my left fist and held the club of my almost useless left arm high so that I could see the damage clearly as I reached into my bag and pulled out the arrow head. Trembling with tension, I pushed the broad barb of the projectile towards the damaged area. It slid between the ribs, the outer edges of the triangular head fitting precisely into the grooves in the bones. Experimentally, I jerked the arrow back in the way I assumed Nephele would have done, trying to escape as the pair of them went over the cliff. The head would not come out as easily as it had gone in. It caught on the inner edges of the curved bones and refused to move. Fascinated, I looked closer still and saw for the first time the marks that ran down the curves from top to bottom, where a knife-point had scored the bones as the arrow-head was cut free. And not any arrow-head either. *This* arrow head. There could be no doubt.

But then it seemed the Goddess herself took a hand, for the way I tugged at the arrow made the skeletal torso move. And, there beneath it, also stripped to the bone, lay a skull. My lamp shed sufficient brightness for me to see at once that it was the skull of a deer, though the antlers had been removed. The lamplight caused something to glitter, however, and I stooped to look closer still. At the place where the antlers had joined the skull were two circular ridges of bone raised the width of my smallest finger above the curve of the cranium. My lamp-flame struck glitters of light from specks of gold in tiny valleys all around the raised bone circles. The antlers might be gone, but some of the gilding still remained on their foundations. Even had the arrow not fitted so neatly between the ribs, I thought, this was proof positive. Proof, like the shattered foreleg, that I could show Odysseus on his return. Breathless, I retrieved the arrow then pulled the skull free. Straightening, I managed to drop them both into my bag before I started to turn.

'Well now, Arouraios,' said a quiet sneering voice behind me, 'It looks as though they were right. Some people just can't let sleeping dogs lie. Or sleeping stags for that matter.'

I straightened fully, gasping with shock, and turned to see two men I had never met before. Yet there was a certain familiarity about them: I knew the tone and the air of menace they brought with them. I had met it that night on the dockside at Troy and had been lucky to survive the encounter. It looked very much as though I was not destined to be so fortunate this time. The speaker, a huge man with the battered face of an unsuccessful pugilist, stepped towards me, pulling a dagger from his belt as he came.

'Convenient place to sort the matter out,' said the second man, Arouraios, a slight rat-faced man with a high, whining voice. 'Won't have to go far to get rid of the body.'

My mind raced, to no effect, flapping like a frightened songbird in a cage. I couldn't throw the lamp at them – my left arm didn't work well enough for that. I couldn't pull out my pretty new dagger because my right hand was still in my bag with the skull and the arrow-head. I couldn't have run from them even if my legs worked properly because I was trapped against the stinking mound of rubbish. I couldn't reason with them – couldn't even beg for mercy – because I felt completely winded and my voice wouldn't work. As though it was my final thought, Odysseus' words popped into my head '*You can't be too careful…*' How true. A lesson I should have learned in Troy.

The massive boxer stepped forward right into the lamplight, a hint of a swagger in his movement. Framed against the shadows and the forest behind, he seemed like some sort of huge gilded statue. The blade of his dagger looked as long as a sword. I was about to close my eyes and accept my fate but I blinked instead. I blinked again. The forest shadows behind my would-be assassin attained form. Substance. Mass. Power. As silently sinister as a great shark closing on a drowning sailor, a huge black bear reared up immediately behind my attacker. His companion saw it and gasped, wide-eyed and wordless. Like me he observed what was happening in a kind of a dream. The bear's long, tooth-lined snout topped the tall man's head. Two huge black-furred arms closed around him until the dagger-long claws on the huge paws met, meshed. The enormous animal tightened its deadly hug. My attacker tried to gasp in his shock; to shout or scream in his abject horror but had no breath to do so. The rat of a companion took to his heels heading one way and I went the other way as fast as I could, dropping the lamp as I did so.

As I ran, over the heaving of my breath and the thunder of my heart I heard a strange, deep grunt and the sound of dead branches being snapped.

No doubt this was the sound that Nephele, priestess of Artemis, also made when all her ribs were crushed.

## 4 - The Second Corpse

i

I staggered blindly through the camp, gasping and choking like a drowning man, lucky not to trip over my weighty bag or any passing guy ropes to go crashing through the tent walls with which I was surrounded. As I ran, I found myself praying that my vision would clear before disaster overtook me. Despite the brightness of the waning moon, the time I had spent looking at the light cast by the lamp-flame deepened the darkness all around. I had almost nothing to guide me except the slope down which I was careering. There was no doubt in my mind that the massive, murderous pugilist was dead, but what if the bear which crushed him was hunting me next? And the rat-faced man, Arouraios, what if he overcame his fright and decided to finish his dead friend's work? I glanced back over my shoulder at the thought, and sure enough, there was his slight but sinister figure flitting from shadow to shadow behind me like something escaped from the underworld. Because he looked like a rat, I had assumed he would be cowardly and only dangerous if cornered like a rat. Another lesson to be spun out of my captain's observations about murderers who didn't look like murderers.

My reasoning so far, such as it was, led on to more jumbled thoughts that came through my panicked mind in the sort of avalanche Poseidon causes from time to time when he shakes the earth. Had Captain Odysseus still been in the camp, I would have gone straight to his tent, calling for help. But disturbing Nestor or Diomedes in the small hours before dawn was simply out of the question, even in this extremity. The thought of Odysseus firmed up my decision as to what I should do, however. If I could not find safety in Odysseus' tent or in those of the kings to whom he had passed responsibility for me during his absence, I could find it back aboard his ship, surrounded by those of his crew he had not taken as his escort on the road to Ithaka. Furthermore, I reasoned, as my panic intensified, *Thalassa* would be the safest place to hide from the murderous Arouraios, leave the tell-tale skull, the broken shank and the arrow; but only if I could find the ship amongst the hulls pulled up onto the beach and get aboard before my lethal little follower caught up with me. Acting captain Eurylocus was a good man to have beside you in a crisis: down-to-earth, practical and not too imaginative. He'd make sure I survived the night if I could get to him. Then I could go and find Diomedes or Nestor in the morning. In the mean-time, fear of my relentless pursuer lent my heels the wings of Hermes. I was running faster than at any time since my disastrous adventure on the dockside at Troy, even if my heaving chest was finding it hard to keep up.

These, then, were the thoughts and impressions that were tumbling through my mind when I collided with a dark figure which suddenly loomed out of the shadows too close in front of me to be avoided. Helplessly, I bounced off him onto a second man who appeared next to him, and went sprawling on the ground, certain that I had just run into Palamedes and Aias, the employers of the crushed giant and the deadly rat so close behind me. I hit the ground, winded, and closed my eyes, preparing to die.

But the voice that asked, with quiet amusement, 'What have we here?' contained no hint of a sneer, nor, blessedly, of a threat.

Neither did the second voice which answered, 'It's Odysseus' rhapsode unless I'm very much mistaken!' A gentle hand took me by my right shoulder and helped me to my feet. As I came up, my vision cleared at last. There was no sign of the hunter who had been so close behind me. Instead, I saw who I had actually run into. Even in the cold silver light of the setting moon, Achilles seemed somehow golden, with Patroclus his slightly dimmer shadow at his side.

'Where are you off to at such speed?' asked the young prince of Phthia.

'Trying to escape an over-zealous worshipper of your excellent epic songs?' suggested Patroclus.

'Or an insensitive and tone-deaf critic, perhaps?' added Achilles.

'Bear,' I gasped. 'There was a bear…'

'A *bear*! Are you sure?' asked Patroclus. 'I only saw a man, and couldn't even be certain of him in amongst all those shadows. Anyway, he's gone now; so's the bear if there ever was one.'

'Have you been wandering about up in the Groves of Artemis?' asked Achilles. 'Surely a bear would hardly dare to come this far out of the forest.'

'No further than the rubbish tips, I'd guess,' nodded Patroclus.

I took a deep breath to steady myself and gasped out to my two princely saviours what had just happened, and what I was planning to do in the immediate future as a consequence.

'*Thalassa*,' said Achilles. 'A wise move and a safe haven – from both bears and rats. We can check up on corpses in the morning. You were wise to run away from the bear and I for one have no intention of running towards one in the dark. But your escape has led you somewhat astray. Had you not bumped into us you would have been amongst the black ships, explaining yourself to my guards. You have been running through the Myrmidon camp.'

\*\*\*

The pre-dawn patrol to check up on their Myrmidon guards that Achilles and Patroclus were undertaking as part of their relentless search for military perfection took them along the beach a good part of the way to *Thalassa* so I was able to accompany them until they could send me safety onwards.

'But you have no idea who was chasing you or why?' asked

Prince Achilles as we set out. 'Only that this pursuer had not been attacked by the bear that killed his colleague and he was called Arouraios…'

'Rat,' said Patroclus. 'More likely to be a nickname than anything a father would call his son. But you felt that Rat and his big friend were waiting for you? Waiting for you to come and look at the carcase of the dead deer?'

'I think so, yes.'

'So someone at the feast must have seen the careful look you gave the carcase as you went past it on your way to your rhapsode's stool,' said Patroclus, who had clearly seen just that himself. 'Someone who knew what deer in fact it was – and that you had been called with Odysseus to discover the name of the man who killed it.'

'Someone astute enough to calculate that you might want to give it a closer inspection in private later on,' added Achilles. 'And to take action accordingly.'

'But someone who had neither the time or the opportunity to make sure the carcase simply vanished,' said Patroclus. 'Someone who therefore sent his two would-be murderers to guard the offal and be ready to kill anyone who got too close to it; in the expectation that if anyone did turn up, it would be you. A very effective trap, when all's said and done, though I'm not quite certain how the murderers were supposed to recognise you. It's unlikely that they were at the High King's feast, so…'

'But almost anybody could order a couple of soldiers to guard a rubbish pile,' I said, hesitant to believe that I was actually important enough to warrant such a lethal scheme. 'And there are fifty thousand of them here, all expecting to be cutting throats before long. So finding a couple happy to cut my throat wouldn't be much of a problem.'

'Almost anybody could send the two soldiers, true; however, only someone at Agamemnon's feast would have seen you giving those ribs a second look,' said Patroclus. Then he shrugged, dismissing his concerns, for the time-being at least. 'But that doesn't get us much further I'm afraid. Twenty or more royal suspects, a physician and a soothsayer, unless the steward, the cook or any of the servants beside the fire had the power and authority to take such action. So, come on then, young man, fill us in on the full details of the affair so far – let's see if that will help us narrow the list of suspects down.'

As we walked from watch-fire to watch-fire checking on the guards, I revealed all the details that Odysseus and I had uncovered, and what the cunning King of Ithaka had reasoned from them.

'But you still have no idea who actually fired the fatal arrow?' asked Achilles when I was finished.

'It looks as though the guilty man must either be Palamedes or Aias,' I said. 'There seems to be no doubt that they delivered the carcase to Agamemnon's steward to be prepared for the feast because he told me they did and he had no reason that I can see to lie. Nor is there any doubt that the carcase they delivered was the one which died alongside the young priestess. The arrow King Odysseus found fits the damage to the ribs, at least one of its forelegs was badly broken as though by a fall from a good height and the skull proves that the antlers were gilded, though they're missing now.'

'That certainly sounds convincing,' nodded Achilles.

'And yet Odysseus and this retired hunter Ikaros were certain only one man was responsible?' probed Patroclus.

'Yes, Highness. There was only one set of hoofprints, one set of footprints and one arrow,' I answered. 'At least only one arrow was found. The dead stag was pulled up into the air and lowered onto the horse in a manner suggesting one man did it, and one set of footprints led the hoofprints of one laden horse away from the clearing where the stag was killed. All the evidence seems to point that way.'

'Again, that seems convincing enough,' allowed Achilles.

'So,' said Patroclus, 'why in the names of all the gods

would Palamedes and Aias get involved if they weren't responsible for killing the deer or the girl? Why risk the wrath of the Goddess and the terrible retribution the High Priestess and the Oracle both say Artemis is demanding?'

'Perhaps,' said Achilles, 'Because neither Palamedes nor Aias has any children. Not even Artemis can make them sacrifice someone who does not exist.'

ii

I stopped, as though struck by one of Zeus' thunderbolts. I had simply not thought of that and I wondered whether Odysseus had. 'But what does that tell us?' I wondered.

'It tells us that whoever killed the girl and the deer knows what the demand of the Goddess in retribution is,' said Achilles. 'Why else choose childless helpers?'

'The whole camp knows that the High Priestess says the Goddess is demanding a life for a life before she will allow us to set sail for Troy,' said Patroclus. His teeth flashed in the shadows as he gave a wry smile. 'I think someone must have told King Nestor. That's all it would take…'

'But,' said Achilles more seriously, 'if Palamedes and Aias gave the carcase to the steward back when the stormy weather began, then there's no guarantee that they knew of the Goddess' judgement. Not that long ago.'

'But,' I speculated. 'What if it was handed over a day or so later?' I racked my brain trying to calculate how long after the priestess' disappearance her body had been found and how long after the murder, therefore, the High Priestess visited her parents, confronted the High King, learned that the body had been found and requested Odysseus' help. For that would have been when the details of the Goddess' curse began to get out.

'But did whoever killed the deer and the priestess know so soon after the act?' wondered Patroclus, breaking into my calculations. 'Did they pass the dead deer on simply hoping to avoid trouble over the young woman's accidental killing –

or were they already suspicious and being careful, therefore, to pass it on to two of the few men who could not be touched by the Goddess' curse?'

'And that,' said Achilles, 'is leaving aside the second part of the Goddess's warning – that none of us are ever going to get to Troy until the appropriate sacrifice is made. Not now and not any time in the future. Even the Myrmidons are getting restless as the full impact of that is beginning to dawn on them, especially as the coincidence of all this bad weather is making the superstitious amongst them believe that Artemis is *really* carrying out the threat the High Priestess and her Oracle say she's made.'

'Only the gods know what it must be doing to the sons of Atreus,' said Patroclus. 'They're both pretty superstitious, so they'll probably half-believe the hand of the Goddess is behind this unseasonal calm so soon after contrary winds and storms. One of them won't get his wife Helen back until this is all sorted out while the other has staked his reputation and fortune on rescuing her for him and destroying the city where she's being held. To the financial benefit of every man here, King, Prince, General, soldier and servant. If they are starting to believe in the curse, then they're both staring ridicule and ruin in the face. Neither would stay enthroned for long after a disappointment like that. Or alive, for that matter.' He paused. 'But I still can't see why Palamedes and Aias have allowed themselves to get caught up in this. They have nothing to lose if we all have to pack up and go home – though, fair enough, they have a certain amount to gain if we all sail soon and Troy falls as quickly as Agamemnon hopes it will.'

'We should go and ask them,' said Achilles.

'I was going to ask King Diomedes to do that in the morning,' I said.

'Hmm,' said Achilles. 'That's a good plan. Perhaps we can leave it to them. We have quite enough to do keeping the Myrmidons sharp and stopping them starting to fight each other and the other armies. For instance, there's bad blood brewing between them and King Menestheus' Athenians for some reason I haven't discovered yet.' He fell silent for an instant, then continued, 'There's *Thalassa*, lad. Off you go then.'

So off I went, thinking *Yes*, it was a good plan. But as things turned out it was a plan doomed to be overtaken by events.

The quickest way from *Thalassa* to King Diomedes' tent ran past Odysseus' empty accommodation. I was hurrying along this route later that morning, laden with what I had discovered last night, full of plans and suggestions, when a familiar figure stepped out from behind the Captain's bivouac right into my path. 'Ikaros,' I said as I recognised the retired hunter and servant of Artemis. 'What are you doing here?'

'Looking for King Odysseus,' said Ikaros. 'But I hear he's gone home to Ithaka.'

'Only for a while,' I answered. 'He'll be back in a few days.'

'Too late,' said the wiry hunter. 'The High Priestess wants him now.'

'Why?' I asked.

'We've found another corpse,' said Ikaros.

\*\*\*

'Another corpse?' I repeated, stunned. 'Where?'

'Just inside the sacred groves, up by the side of the road to Thebes. It's one of your people this time.'

'What do you mean?'

'It's no-one from the temple or from Aulis as far as we can fathom – but you'd be a good judge of that, being a local lad. He looks like some sort of messenger. Military; courtly maybe. There's an arrow in his side and his throat's been cut. Someone wanted to make absolutely certain he was dead by the look of it. High Priestess Karpathia is with your High King now. To be fair she would have been down to see him in any case to find out how the investigation into Nephele's death is going. It's been a good few days now. Have you heard anything in the meantime?'

'Agamemnon handed it over to Prince Palamedes in Odysseus' absence. Palamedes has recruited his friend Prince Aias to help him. I haven't heard anything more than that.'

'Karpathia won't like that. She was impressed by Odysseus and you. As was I.'

'Impressed by *me*? She hardly noticed me. It was all Odysseus and you. I was just stumbling along in your footsteps.'

'She didn't see it that way. I think she'd want me to take you to her. If she can't have the master, maybe his man will do. We left the corpse precisely as we found it on the assumption Odysseus would want to see it before it was moved. Can you come with me now?'

I hesitated. 'I was just on my way to see King Diomedes,' I explained. 'I discovered something last night I thought he should know about and I was going to ask him what to do about the man that the bear killed.'

'The man the bear killed...' echoed the hunter his tone hovering somewhere between shock and scepticism.

In a few words I explained what had happened, why, and what I had discovered.

'We'll go and examine the site,' he decided. 'Whether there's a man killed by a bear there or not, I want to see that carcase too. Fair enough, if we have the head and hoof in your bag along with the arrow King Odysseus found, then that all adds up to a pretty convincing case. But the more I see for myself, the more use I'll be to the High Priestess. Let's go!'

Side by side we hurried through the stirring camp, doing our best to avoid the soldiers as they went about their business, washing, visiting latrines and consuming their meagre battlefield breakfast. At least the bustle thinned as we approached the rubbish piles. This was hardly surprising. The cess pits were some distance away and there was nothing in bowls of gruel, loaves of coarse emmer bread and pots of olive oil or honey that needed to be thrown away – not by thousands of bored and hungry soldiers willing to consume every last crumb or drop. So Ikaros and I approached the pile I had visited last night absolutely alone.

'This is it?' Ikaros asked, looking up as we arrived.

'Yes.'

'I can't see any bears. That's a good start.'

I dismissed his jocularity, for not only could I not see any bears, I couldn't see any corpses. Nor, when I rounded the stinking mound, could I see the dead deer's bones either.

'It's gone,' I said.

'Good thing too,' he answered, still thinking I was talking about the bear.

'No,' I said urgently. 'Not just the bear. The body, the carcase, everything!'

He opened his mouth and I could see the question trembling on his lips – *Are you sure this is the right mound?* But the question never came. At least part of the reason for that must have been the fact that we had been following my tracks – cautious footprints coming up, reckless ones going back down. And this was the place they stopped. And started. A frown flashed across his face. 'So someone's been here and cleared the mess away,' he said quietly. 'Lots of footprints over there.' He gestured to the far side of the mound where the Rat had appeared and disappeared last night. 'Your rat-faced man and his friends I would guess. But I doubt they'd have cleared away everything that men like you and I can see...'

He went down on one knee and bent towards the ground, sniffing. 'I smell blood,' he said, glancing up at me. He put his spread palm on the grass and raised it for me to see. It was red and covered thickly. 'Almost as much blood here as there was from the stag's slit throat,' he said. 'And the prints of a bear's paws. Biggest I've ever seen. Looks like the Rat's friend was either torn to pieces, or he burst like an overblown bladder.'

iii

'Right,' said Ikaros after a brief, thoughtful pause. 'I never doubted you but this proves your story. Let's take everything you've discovered to my Basilissa the High Priestess.' He straightened, giving a bark of cynical laughter. 'She and the High King were on bad enough terms already. What will happen when she finds out he actually ate the sacred deer I can't imagine!'

'I ate some of it myself,' I admitted nervously.

'Let's not mention that,' he said. 'And let's hope the Goddess didn't notice it either or you could find yourself in trouble too. Right. Wait here and I'll scout along the trail left by the bear, up as far as the edge of the forest at least, I won't be long.'

'But why?'

'It could have been the bear that took the corpse of the man it killed. Or, more importantly, it could have taken the carcase of the deer. It would have been down here foraging for food after all!' And with that, he was off.

I stood, waiting listlessly, my mind wandering through forests of speculation, hardly aware of my surroundings at all – despite the stench, the flies and the hungry birds, cats and dogs, all foraging like the bear had done.

'*So,*' said Arouraios the Rat, his voice sliding into my thoughts like a dagger between ribs. 'They were right. Here you are back again. You just can't keep away, can you?'

I swung round to face him, mouth hanging open, simply aghast.

'And by the look of things you have kindly brought everything I'm looking for. I'll wager you have the missing skull in that bag. And I see you have the tell-tale dagger in your belt. Just too much temptation to be resisted...'

I was quicker thinking this morning. The gaudy gift was

out before he finished speaking, its bright blade pointed straight at him.

'Oh,' he chuckled. 'So you want to make a fight of it this time, do you?' He pulled out his own dagger and flung himself forward. The action was so immediate and unexpected after his drawling speech it caught me completely off guard. His dagger knocked mine aside and was within a finger-length of my side when there was a *crack*! That sounded disturbingly like a breaking rib. Rat's head was flung sideways and his body followed it, collapsing onto the slope of the rubbish tip. He lay still. A trickle of blood began to run down his face from just above his cheekbone in front of the top of his ear and a big bruise started to form around it.

'I take it that's the Rat,' said Ikaros, coiling his sling round his fingers as he approached.

'Is he dead?' I wondered.

'I doubt it. You want to slit his throat? That's twice now. He's hunting you and he knows what you look like.'

'He knows what this dagger looks like at any rate,' I said, stooping to pick it up.' I held the gaudy weapon up. 'I was given it for reciting an epic song last night.'

'A double-edged gift if potential murderers can use it to identify you,' said Ikaros pensively. As he talked, he stooped and retrieved the Rat's dagger too, holding it up to examine the blade. It was clearly an old weapon, well-used, though recently honed. The edge of the bronze blade had become serrated through clashes with other daggers over the years and the Rat had clearly sought to make use of this, turning part of the edge into a kind of saw. Ikaros fell silent for a moment longer as he examined this, then he continued, 'Well, we'll have to leave him here, alive or dead. We can't go wandering about the place with him slung over our shoulders. And we've got to get on. The High Priestess is no more patient than the Goddess is.' He paused for a moment, looking down at the unconscious man then he handed me the

Rat's dagger. 'I don't know,' he said. 'That was a very near thing. Maybe the Goddess noticed that you ate some of her sacred deer after all.'

I looked at the dagger he had just given me, unsure what to do with it. 'Stick it in your belt and hide the jewelled one away,' he advised. 'You appear to be in enough trouble with the Goddess without adding anyone to the list who's been ordered like Rat here, to kill the man with the limp and the gaudy knife.'

We walked silently through the camp, side by side as I slid Agamemnon's dagger into the bag beside the arrow, the foreleg and the skull. There were questions trembling on the tip of my tongue but I was hesitant to voice them. Ikaros seemed such a practical man – very much of the earthly realm rather than the celestial, despite his position in the Temple of Artemis. Like acting captain Eurylocus of *Thalassa* but rather more imaginative. How was it, therefore, that he talked about the Goddess as though she was not only real but closely involved in the doings of mere mortals like us? It struck me as an attitude which was strikingly different to Odysseus' and that was unsettling because they were so similar in other ways. Did I dare ask him the double-edged question that seemed to be at the heart of this affair – is the Goddess really controlling the weather and stopping the High King's army sailing to Troy? If she is, will she continue to do so until the guilty man is unmasked and the terrible sacrifice made? I found myself shivering slightly at the thought of such a powerful and implacable being becoming so closely involved in our seemingly insignificant lives. How dangerous was it for Odysseus and me that the vital task of unmasking the man who had killed Artemis' priestess – leading to the satisfaction of her horrific demands - apparently lay almost entirely in the hands of my captain and myself?

\*\*\*

By the greatest of good fortune, Ikaros was content to let us go to the High King's tent and our meeting with the High

Priestess via Diomedes' accommodation. The King of Argos had finished his morning rituals and was free to join us before he went to exercise his troops. In as few words as possible, I explained what was going on and long before I had finished, the young king had joined us so that we three arrived at Agamemnon's tent shoulder to shoulder. We were stopped at the entrance by a squad of guards who, although respectfully apologetic, refused to let even the king enter. As we waited, I could hear raised voices from inside. The High Priestess, the High King and someone else were clearly having a discussion about dangerous matters.

Part-way through this increasingly heated debate, Palamedes and Aias arrived together with a servant who had clearly been sent to summon them. The two princes pushed arrogantly past us as though we were too lowly to merit their attention – let alone their courtesy. The guards parted to allow them entry and as they did so, Diomedes led Ikaros and myself through in their footsteps as though leading a charge against the Scaean Gate of Troy itself. The guards hesitated. Stopping us as we arrived was clearly one thing – barring our way as we pushed through in the princes' footsteps was another.

We found the High Priestess Karpathia alone in the reception area facing the High King and his brother Menelaus. One glance assured me that the High Priestess didn't need any support; no earthly support at any rate. 'Here,' said Agamemnon as Palamedes and Aias entered. 'In the absence of your choice King Odysseus, here are the men looking into the matter!' Such was his obvious anger that he did not appear to notice we three following behind them, though this could also be because we hesitated in the outer lobby.

Karpathia swung round to face the two princes. 'And what have you discovered?' she snapped to Palamedes. 'King Odysseus discovered how the girl died, how the stag died, how her body was hidden and how its carcase was transported away all within an afternoon! What more have you discovered in the days that have passed since he left?'

'Nothing more,' said Palamedes, his tone making clear that he was mightily insulted to be addressed in such an abrupt manner.

'No further towards discovering who fired the fatal arrow?'

'No.'

'No further towards discovering where the stag with the golden antlers is being hidden?'

'No!'

'That's funny,' said Ikaros, stepping forward and interrupting as though he was talking to a beggar rather than a prince. 'Because you all ate it last night!'

A silence descended as though Zeus the Thunderer was hovering just above us. Diomedes and I also stepped into the reception area to stand behind Ikaros and Karpathia.

'Who is this?' grated Agamemnon, glaring at the retired huntsman.

'His name is Ikaros,' snapped Karpathia. 'He is one of my servants!'

'Why am I not surprised?' demanded Agamemnon in a mock-fainting voice.

'And has your servant any proof of this allegation?' demanded Palamedes.

'I...' I began, stepping forward - only to find myself pushed firmly back by Ikaros.

Diomedes also stepped forward as though hiding me behind his more massive frame. 'There was ample proof,' he said. 'It was up on the rubbish mound last night where the High King's cooks put it after the feast. But it has gone.'

'I see...' Palamedes voice lingered on the word. He exchanged a glance with Aias. Was there a tinge of relief in his expression, I wondered. 'Gone. Yes, I see...' he continued silkily.

'You are not the only one that sees,' snarled Karpathia. 'The Goddess sees!' She swept the four men opposite her with a withering glance. 'You can lie to us but you cannot lie to her. And don't for a heartbeat suppose that she will sit idly by in the face of your sneering and evasion. I warn you, if you persist in this secrecy and equivocation, you will find the hand of the Goddess in more than just the weather which is doing so much damage to you and your plans!' She turned on her heel and stormed out, leaving Diomedes, Ikaros and me with no choice but to follow her.

iv

'Basilissa,' said Ikaros, humbly, as the High Priestess stalked down the hill from Agamemnon's tent towards Aulis and her chariot. 'I had supposed you planned to ask the High King about the new corpse…'

'I did so,' answered Karpathia. 'The pompous fool and his cuckold brother deny any knowledge of any man who might be found murdered on the road to Thebes, what he was doing there or how he came to die there but of course they are lying. Their duplicity is written plainly on their faces!' She took a deep breath. 'So our conversation moved rather rapidly onto the central matter that lies between us. The murder of my priestess and the sacred deer, and the utter failure of the men he has appointed to look into it to discover anything important at all.' She took another, calming breath, then continued, more moderately. 'But I see that in the absence of King Odysseus you have brought his right hand. Good. And I assume from the speed with which you silenced him that he has the proof of the allegation you made. Though I have to admit I was not surprised to hear that the deer has been eaten. Why else kill it? Hardly for a pair of gilded antlers after all! And King Diomedes, I'm sure the Goddess is very flattered to find you offering your help as well.'

'I doubt whether I can replace King Odysseus in any meaningful way,' said Diomedes.

'Highness,' said Ikaros, 'It seems to me that you will be doing service enough if you just keep the rhapsode here alive.

Whether the Rat is dead or alive, he was certainly not working alone and he was clearly tasked with stopping Odysseus' investigation from going any further – even though Odysseus was not investigating in person for the moment. Just as our young rhapsode seems to have impressed more powerful people than he realised, he has obviously also managed to make many more powerful enemies than he dreams of.'

'I see what you mean,' said Diomedes. 'And of all the men most likely to be responsible for setting the Rat on his mission, those four must head the list. Well, three of them at any rate – I can't see where poor old Menelaus could possibly fit into the pattern such as it is.'

'Unless,' suggested Ikaros, 'Menelaus is as willing as the guilty man to cover everything up in the hope that the invasion can proceed at once and he can recover his errant wife from Prince Paris' harem all the sooner.'

'However,' I added, 'Just before he left for Ithaka, King Odysseus suggested to me that the High King has appointed Palamedes and Aias to your investigation precisely because he does not want the matter resolved. Whoever fired the fatal arrow is likely to have been one of the leaders of the army; no-one else would be up there hunting alone. Agamemnon simply dare not order such a man to bring his family here and then sacrifice a child to satisfy the Goddess. It would destroy his plans and ruin his standing; and, as even Prince Achilles has observed, it could conceivably start a civil war.' I would have added *especially as neither Odysseus or he really believe the Goddess is as directly involved as everyone at her temple seems to be*. But perhaps wisely, I held my tongue.

'But the Goddess must be satisfied,' said Karpathia, proving my mental point at once. 'If she is not, the entire campaign will stop. Not only stop, but never, ever, proceed. Even if he tries again in ten years' time, he will get no further than Aulis until the sacrifice is made. What will that do to the High King's standing and reputation?'

'Nothing good, that's for certain,' said Diomedes. 'He's in a cleft stick. He dare not have the guilty man unmasked in case that starts a war between the armies here. But the armies know how the situation needs to be resolved – by revealing the murderer and sacrificing his child. If Agamemnon does not unmask the guilty man and demand the sacrifice, then they are quite likely to turn on him. And his brother as likely as not because Menelaus and his flighty wife started this whole mess. That would offer a kind of neatness I suppose – the man who started it all and his brother the man who cannot finish it in the manner he had planned and promised. Agamemnon and Menelaus would either be killed or forced to run and hide. Then the armies, carrying their generals along with them, would start to look for a new leader who is not held back by the hand of the Goddess and who, therefore, can take them to Troy, riches and glory.'

'The armies would do this? The common soldiers?' asked the High Priestess.

'Certainly. Unless their kings and generals can hold them back. Achilles could, I could, Nestor could, well his sons could; Odysseus obviously could, Ajax could – he could probably do it on his own he's so huge. But other than half a dozen more who have been staying on top of their troops, the rest wouldn't stand much of a chance if the armies turned against them.'

'Interesting,' said Karpathia. 'That is a dynamic I had not considered. I must discuss it with Pythia and see what the Oracle has to say. But the first thing we must do is to find out who the new corpse was when he lived and, if possible, why he died. He lies in the Groves of the Goddess and we simply cannot ignore that fact. It is even possible that the Goddess in some way called him to herself and allowed him to be discovered on sacred ground in order to move matters forward out of this impasse. Do you wish to accompany us, King Diomedes?'

'At first I thought not. The conversation we have just

enjoyed has emphasised to me quite forcefully that I should be hard at work making sure my four thousand Argive soldiers know precisely who commands them and how vital it is for them to obey his orders. But now I'm not so sure. Whether or not the Goddess is using us all as her puppets as you say, there is something going on here that doesn't feel right and in the absence of Odysseus, I think I'd better offer whatever extra assistance I can.'

***

I was allowed the privilege of riding in King Diomedes' chariot which, like Odysseus', was stabled in Aulis. It was spacious, but much less so than the High Priestess' vehicle which had plenty of room for a charioteer, the High Priestess and her two attendants to fit comfortably aboard. It was pulled by two strong horses but at a speed which allowed Ikaros and a couple of guards to lope alongside as we left Aulis on the road to Thebes. Diomedes' charioteer kept his horses on a tight rein so that we could travel alongside the High Priestess' slower vehicle, allowing the conversations to continue. As we made our leisurely way out of the city towards the turning that led up through the trees to the temple, I explained in detail what I had found out and how the contents of my bulky leather bag supported what I believed. A bumpy ride in a jolting carriage was no time or place to show the High Priestess bits of broken bone and gilded skull, so Karpathia said she would be content to take my word for it until we reached the temple and she could see for herself.

We arrived at the temple soon after noon. The day, like all the others recently, was windless and blazingly hot, however the road we were following through the trees towards the temple proved shady enough to rob the fearsome sun of some of its crushing power. And, although down amongst the foothills and on the plains beside the coast there was a dead calm, a gentle pine-fragrant breeze moved through the forest up here, helping the shadows to keep us cool to such good effect that Diomedes remarked upon it. 'The breath of the Goddess,' explained Karpathia. 'She looks after her own.'

Nevertheless, a bowl of fresh spring water was very welcome as we assembled in the temple's reception area after we had left the chariots outside. Welcome also were the bread and honey that the temple's bakery and hives produced – though I preferred the fragrant olive oil that was also on offer together with the sharp sheep's cheese the servants made from their flock's excess milk. I was particularly glad of the food because I had eaten nothing since the bone-spiked venison at Agamemnon's feast last night. However, no sooner had we refreshed ourselves than Diomedes, Ikaros and I were off again, leaving my bag and its contents for Karpathia to examine at her leisure.

We took Diomedes' chariot. The king and I rode in it along with the charioteer, while the temple guards who had accompanied Karpathia back from Aulis ran alongside, led by Ikaros who guided us with terse instructions. We were soon back on the road to Thebes, heading up-hill away from Aulis. Ikaros and the guards ran on the inside of the chariot along the edge of the road. The highway cut through the forested slopes, the trees standing tall on either hand, the ground between their trunks covered with undergrowth – mostly of bushes hardy enough to withstand the constant gentle rain of pine-needles. Under the heat of the early afternoon, the thoroughfare was by no means busy. Only the occasional cart or pack-animal led by a weary trader disturbed the whining hum of the summer-hot copses. There was a subtle difference between the woodland on our left and that on our right. To our right, the thickets were quiet. They were as full of wild-life as those on our left no doubt, but the heat of early afternoon seemed to have struck everything dumb and stunned it into restfulness. On our left, however, the Groves of Artemis were gently a-bustle. Insects buzzed and whined; cicadas sang drowsily. Birds fluttered and called. Creatures scurried, snuffled and whispered. The cool, fragrant breath of the Goddess no doubt helped, but it seemed to blow more constantly in the sacred stands than elsewhere.

Just as we crested the first low rise and caught a glimpse of the all-but empty roadway reaching down into the first shady valley between here and Thebes, Ikaros said, 'Here.' Diomedes' charioteer pulled right to the side of the road and reined to a stop. Diomedes and I dismounted and fell in with Ikaros and the guards, leaving the charioteer to tend his horses. The retired huntsman led us a little distance away from the road into the first of the shadily stirring thickets. We didn't need to go far and we didn't need to strain our woodsmanship to follow the tracks through the undergrowth that showed where something had been dragged deeper. The footprints suggested two men.

'One man holding each arm,' said Ikaros. 'Dragging him in here to hide him.'

'He must have been dead then,' said Diomedes. 'There's no sign of him struggling.'

'The arrow might have killed him,' nodded Ikaros. 'Or they might have cut his throat by the roadside I haven't looked there in any detail as yet.'

'We'll do that later, then,' said Diomedes.

'But we have to look here most closely first,' said Ikaros, pulling aside a bush to reveal the corpse of a man lying flat on his back with an arrow sticking out of his armpit and a gaping slit in his throat that stretched from one ear to the other.


v

The corpse was that of a middle-aged man. His hair was grey and thinning, his eyebrows shaggy and his beard trimmed short – which went some way to explaining why his cut throat was so striking. His wide eyes were filmed. They struck me as being those of a blind man, but when I mentioned this with some surprise given the circumstances, Ikaros said that the eyes of the dead clouded over if they were not shut; it was true of animals and of men alike. It was also worth noting, he suggested, that the covering of bushes had protected the eyes – blind or not – from the beaks of the local birds. The clothing beneath the cut throat was covered in blood and that was providing a feast for the local ant and insect population, some of which had climbed into the wound itself and seemed reluctant to move, even when Ikaros waved them away. The stained clothing was a travelling outfit of himation, cloak and thick leggings suggesting he had been travelling on horseback. There seemed little doubt of that, and marks on the inner curves of the leggings also suggested that the dead man had been riding; something that a blind man was not likely to be doing. The condition of his left arm, shoulder and side seemed consistent with damage sustained falling sideways off a horse as the result of receiving an arrow just behind his right arm, so close to the limb and at such an angle as to suggest that it had almost pierced the arm-pit itself. It must have hit with considerable force to knock the rider off his seat I thought. 'I see what you meant when you said to the High Priestess that this must have been a messenger,' I said.

'But from whom, to whom, and bearing what message?' wondered Diomedes.

Something in the young king's tone alerted me. 'Do you recognise him, Majesty?'

Diomedes pulled a face and shook his head, more in frustration than in answer to my question. After a moment more, Ikaros, Diomedes and I all knelt around the corpse. As it was clear that the king had never undertaken a task like this, Ikaros and I took the lead. The gentle breeze was strong enough to move the branches so that shafts of sunlight swept regularly across the dead man's face and body, making every element easy to see, though of course those details remained much less easy to understand.

Trying to recall as many details as I could of how Odysseus went about such tasks, I leaned forward, examining the dead face. There was nothing there that called out to me except, perhaps, the manner in which blood had collected and thickened on the bearded jowls beneath the chin, making a black-floored, white speckled hillock joining the lower jaw to the sundered neck and suggesting that the man had been lying on his back when his throat was cut – the blood spurting upwards and downwards with equal force. After the arrow knocked him off the horse, therefore, but before it actually killed him.

I next examined the throat, remembering Odysseus' dictum *'Eyes first and most, hands last and least.'* I did not touch the wound therefore, but examined it as closely as I was able, disregarding the ants and flies. Seeing instead the manner in which the skin had been cut – almost torn. How the wound stretched wide from one ear to the other; proof again that two men must have been involved – one to hold the head still while the other did this to the throat – as he lay helpless and dying on his back. A vigorous man cutting the gullet; a strong man therefore holding the head still as the deed was done. The manner in which the various tubes and vessels had been torn loose was striking but I could not immediately fathom any reason why it should be so unless it was simply a result of the vigorous chopping, slicing and sawing. There was no doubt in my mind, however; they had been pulled loose as well as being chopped apart. The blade that had done this had cut right through to the muscles of the neck before it had stopped, revealing glimpses of white bone from the spine.

'Were they trying to behead him?' wondered Ikaros, his voice making me jump, quiet though it was.

'Why would anyone do such a thing?' wondered Diomedes.

'Proof that they'd done their job,' said Ikaros. 'It's not uncommon.'

'But they gave up.' I observed. 'I wonder why.'

'Probably too difficult – whatever they used had just hit solid muscle and bone after all. Or maybe they ran out of time

– even getting this far must have taken a good while. Or on the other hand, someone was maybe coming along the road – perhaps the murder was done at a busier time.' Ikaros ticked off the possibilities.

'I wonder where they did it, though,' I said. 'It can't have been here. No blood on the ground…'

'Unlike the grass by the rubbish tip this morning' nodded Ikaros. 'Yes, you're right.'

'Surely it would have to be at the beginning of the track you followed here,' suggested Diomedes. 'Have you examined the undergrowth by the roadside there?'

'No. maybe we'll do that later,' said Ikaros. 'But we need to press on here for the moment.'

'Well,' I said, 'unless we're planning to strip him, there's not a lot more to examine. The arrow's just about in his right arm-pit, though there's not much blood there I notice. Judging by what's sticking out, the point is in very deep indeed. Fired at close range – maybe just across the width of the road. His arm was raised, elbow forward – as it would be holding reins. And, unless the killers are being particularly devious, everything suggests that he was riding west, towards Thebes.'

'It certainly looks that way,' agreed Ikaros.

'But who was he?' said Diomedes, almost talking to himself, still obviously frustrated not to be able to remember where he knew the face from.

And as chance would have it, I was able to answer that question a few moments later when I held his dead right hand up beside my living one so that the king and the huntsman could compare the identical calluses on our fingertips and thumb. 'He was a rhapsode,' I said.

'Of course!' said Diomedes. 'How could I not see it immediately? How could I not have known at once? This is the man you replaced at the feast last night, lad. This is Sophos, High King Agamemnon's rhapsode!'

***

King Diomedes' revelation altered everything. The three of us sat back on our heels silently regarding each-other as our minds whirled. The first thing that occurred to me was that Agamemnon must have been lying to the High Priestess. But then I realised… 'The High King hasn't actually seen the body. All he knows is what the High Priestess told him,' I said.

'True,' agreed Ikaros. 'And I described to her a man of middle years in travelling clothes who had been shot with an arrow and who had then had his throat cut…'

'That could have been almost anybody,' I observed, and Ikaros nodded ruefully.

'But when did you estimate that the murder took place?' wondered the king.

'Quite recently…'

'Within a day or two?' I queried. 'His clothes are bone dry. This was done after the weather changed. Soon after, perhaps, but not too soon – he must have fallen onto ground that was also bone-dry.'

'So that Agamemnon might well have assumed his rhapsode could not be the man, especially if he was sent some days earlier – soon after the moment the weather changed perhaps.'

'That's right. I seem to remember that Sophos left just before Odysseus, in fact. But where was he sent? With what purpose?' wondered Diomedes.

'Sent to Mycenae,' I answered. 'With a message. Odysseus said that messengers have been going back and forth between the High King and Queen Clytemnestra. This must have been a longer, more intricate message than usual, though. I've come across this before. Anyone wishing to send a lengthy, complicated message – especially if he expects a long, complicated reply - can do no better than to get his rhapsode to memorise it.'

'Just as he memorises lengthy epic songs, word for word. Yes, I see,' breathed Diomedes.

'It has to be a message for Queen Clytemnestra then,' said Ikaros. 'But who would want to stop the High King communicating with his queen?'

'I think we're going to have to show him the corpse and then ask him ourselves,' said Diomedes.

'That's one way forward, I suppose,' said Ikaros uneasily.

But in the end it was the way we chose.

As the two guards loaded the corpse into Diomedes' chariot, Ikaros studied the roadside at the end of the tracks left when Sophos was dragged deeper into the woods. Sure enough, there were bloodstains here, but unlike those by the rubbish pile this morning, these were completely dry. 'When did the weather change?' he asked, talking to himself. 'Six days ago? Could it be seven?'

'Just before Odysseus went west,' I said, 'and he's due back soon, I think.'

The conversation stopped there, except that Ikaros ran across the road and searched for the place from which the ambush had been launched. 'Here!' he called after a few moments. 'Two men judging by the footprints – but that doesn't get us any further. We already knew two men were involved.'

And that was all, except that as I climbed aboard Diomedes chariot again I realised that Karpathia still had my bag full of the evidence I wanted to show King Odysseus as soon as he did get back. 'Don't worry,' said Ikaros. 'The High Priestess and the Oracle will take good care of it and when they've finished with it, I'll bring it back to you myself. If Odysseus is back before then I'll look to find you at his tent. If not, you'll likely be aboard *Thalassa*. Don't worry. I'll find you, and I won't need to have you holding some brightly jewelled dagger to do it!'

'As you wish,' I said, realising I had little choice in the matter. Diomedes would be hesitant to go back to the Temple as it was a good deal out of his way; and, as Ikaros had already observed, there was no guarantee that the High

Priestess would be ready to return it if he did.

'It just shows you though,' said Ikaros as a kind of parting shot while the charioteer stirred the horses into motion and the wheels rolled forward, leaving the hunter and the temple guards standing by the roadside, 'if the High Priestess was able to describe the High King's rhapsode to him and the High King didn't recognise who she was talking about, how important was that unique and unmistakable dagger the High King gave to you.'

As Diomedes and I rode eastwards again, back down towards Aulis and the huge camp that stood beside it with the corpse of Sophos lying at our feet, I said, 'Do you think Ikaros was right, Highness? Did King Agamemnon give me the dagger simply so that I would be easy to recognise?' My voice shook a little, for I was finding it very hard to come to terms with the potentially fatal notoriety that had been so suddenly thrust upon me.

'About that,' said Diomedes. 'You know, I'm not certain that it was actually the High King who gave the dagger to Oikonomos the steward. There were several people gathered around there at the time. Menelaus, for instance, as well as Palamedes, Aias, King Menestheus and King Leonteus. It would have been easy for any one of them to give Oikonomos the dagger and say it came from Agamemnon himself.'

This silenced me for the rest of the journey as I pondered a widened pool of suspects who might want me dead and wondered whether or not I should be relieved that the short-tempered, ruthless and all-powerful Agamemnon was no longer the only one on the list.

## 5 - The Rat and the Rhapsode

i

As we approached Aulis' western gate, King Diomedes spoke quietly to his charioteer and we turned off the main highway onto the hard-beaten earth track that was effectively the inland road to the Achaean army's vast camp. 'Where are we going, Majesty?' I asked.

'We're taking the corpse to the most logical destination,' said Diomedes. 'The quarters of Prince Machaon and Prince Podialirius the camp physicians. They will be able to examine it further. They are both accomplished surgeons and will be able to remove the arrow with any luck so that we can compare that with the one which killed the priestess when Karpathia returns it to you. Then they can have the body stripped, washed and prepared to be handed to Kalkhas for proper funeral rights, unless Karpathia decides to claim him on behalf of the Goddess because he was killed and hidden in the Groves of Artemis. And somewhere in all this preparation, we will bring the High King over to give formal identification to the corpse which he swore could have nothing to do with him.'

'I would like to witness that moment,' I said.

'A dangerous wish,' warned the young king. 'It seems you are in sufficient danger as things stand. To witness the High King taken in a lie might well have fatal consequences – even more immediate and certain than those apparently hanging over you now.'

I fell silent, still finding it difficult to believe that someone as insignificant as a partially crippled and half-blind rhapsode could possibly be of sufficient importance to merit murder on the command of a High King. But then, I considered, the situation was merely a lesser reflection of what seemed to be going on here and now: that the doings of such insignificant creatures as men could possibly merit the personal outrage of a Goddess who lived in far, high Olympus.

I was still pondering these unsettling questions when the chariot drew up beside the brother physicians' accommodation. At first glance, it seemed strange that the physicians should have needed not one great tent, but several. It was only when Diomedes and I entered the main one that I realised the truth. Even now, when the army was effectively at rest, there were still soldiers who were unwell, hurt and wounded. The range of aliments could be identified with a glance. Sickness arising from all the usual sources as well as from unwisely-foraged, spoiled and ill-prepared food. Accidents suffered during training; cuts and bruises, stabs and gashes arising from fights of all kinds from mock battles and competitive wrestling matches to knock-down drag-out brawls. Thousands of short-tempered, bored and frustrated fighting men cooped up together with dwindling supplies and no immediate prospect of getting into action: it was a wonder to me that there weren't many more in here awaiting the physicians' attention. But the tent did not appear to be packed and I assumed that the neighbouring ones were likewise less than full, though the physicians and their helpers clearly had quite a lot to do, passing out medicines, tending broken bones and binding wounds.

As chance would have it, however, poor Sophos was their first corpse; at least that was what the servant who greeted us said before arranging for the body to be carried in and then scurrying off to summon his masters. This fact alone called both of them in to view it mere moments after our arrival. Like many heroes, including Achilles and my own captain Odysseus, Machaon and his brother Podialirius had been tutored by the wise and ancient Chiron on Mount Pelion; travelling from their great fortress of Larisa, capital of their kingdom of Thessaly just as, one generation earlier, their father King Asclepius had done before them. It was by no means a long journey for Pelion was within the borders of their kingdom and perhaps that was why the three of them, father and sons, had all spent more time with the elderly teacher than almost any others of his students.

As he did with Achilles and his father King Peleus of neighbouring Phthia, Chiron taught the Thessalian father and then the sons not only the arts of hunting, woodcraft and warfare but also those of healing. Achilles, I knew, would have made a fine physician had he not found himself to be the greatest warrior of his generation – perhaps of all time. Asclepius, on the other hand excelled in the medical field and ensured that his sons did also. Thus, as well as leading the Thessalian army, brought here in thirty ships, amongst the first to arrive, they were the men all the other leaders turned to in matters of medicine and surgery. Which was precisely what Diomedes was doing now.

The brother physicians could hardly have been less alike. Machaon was a square, commanding figure with a virile beard, curly hair and the largest hands I had ever seen – and I had seen Ajax's. Podialirius in contrast was slim, beardless, fair hair like thistledown receding at the front and thinning on the crown. His hands were smaller than his brother's, long-fingered and delicate. But both men had piercing brown eyes which had the ability apparently to see below the surface or through the skin and look straight into you, body and mind. Something they had in common not only with each other but also with Odysseus.

*\*\**

Machaon had been at last night's feast, and many others before that for he and Podialirius had been amongst the earliest to answer Agamemnon's call to arms. He had enjoyed not only the High King's food, therefore, but also his entertainment. Unlike Diomedes, he had no trouble in recognising the dead man lying on the table in front of him. 'This is Sophos!' he said, clearly shocked. 'Who has dared to do this to the High King's rhapsode?'

'That's what we're trying to find out,' said Diomedes. 'Do you think you and Podialirius can cut out the arrow? We have another one we wish to compare it with.'

The physician looked up, narrow-eyed, his face set. 'With the arrow that killed the priestess and the sacred deer I suppose,' he said.

'Just so,' answered Diomedes.'

'I thought the High Priestess asked Odysseus to look into that matter and the High King then deputed Palamedes in Odysseus' absence!' There was the briefest of pauses, then Machaon continued, 'But one glance tells me that the arrow did not kill poor Sophos. The cut throat did and this excess of blood proves it.'

'True,' said Diomedes. 'But we calculate that this was only because the throat was cut mere moments after the arrow hit – before in fact, it had a real chance to do its work. For I'm sure you will agree that it would have killed him quickly enough had the throat not been cut.' As Diomedes was explaining our thinking in this matter, Machaon's gaze raked over me – prompted no doubt by the prince's use of the word 'we'.

'And so savagely cut!' added Podialirius, apparently the gentler of the two brothers. 'As he lay helpless on his back on the ground by the look of it. To what purpose?' He shook his head sadly.

'We thought, perhaps, that the killer planned to take his head as proof of a task completed,' said Diomedes.

'Though it does seem a strong possibility,' I emphasised, without thinking – despite the fact that I was interrupting a conversation between a king and two princes, 'that the murderers just needed the matter settled swiftly and didn't have time to wait for the arrow to kill him outright.'

'But whatever knife they used,' continued Diomedes, 'It certainly wasn't up to the job of taking the head off after the throat was cut and the murder accomplished.'

'No knife would be,' said Machaon, his interest caught. He

moved the rhapsode's head from side to side with some difficulty, demonstrating the thickness of the muscles joining the skull to the shoulders, matched by the strength of the spinal column that they supported. 'It would take a powerful stroke from an extremely sharp sword or, better still, an axe. I suppose the murderer thought at first his knife was up to the job.'

'Why would that be?' wondered Diomedes. 'Surely any man who is soldier enough to be here in Aulis would be aware of the limitations of a dagger under such circumstances.'

'I would guess that he may have calculated – wrongly, as we can see – that the fact his weapon had some kind of saw-blade might give him sufficient advantage,' mused Machaon.

'Saw-blade, Majesty?' I queried.

'Yes, lad. You can tell from the skin at the edges of the wound, the torn strings of muscle at the front of the neck and the manner in which the tubes have been pulled loose as well as being cut through. And, if you observe closely, the marks on the muscles themselves. This was done with quite an unusual blade. It was not merely a straight edge, honed sharp. It also had at least in some part, a series of serrations that meant it could be used not only to stab, cut and slice, but also to saw.' He moved one massive fist beside the gaping wound, demonstrating how such a blade might be employed – and giving a graphic demonstration of how the various tubes and vessels had been sundered. Tearing loose as they yielded to the sideways sawing motion.

Gripped by something between a suspicion and a certainty so strong that it almost knocked the wind out of me, I pulled the Rat's dagger out of my belt and held it up for the princely physician to see. 'A blade like this one?' I asked. The light caught the serrations down one edge of the long blade, that turned it into a saw indeed.

'Yes,' said Machaon. 'Exactly like that one.'

ii

'So,' said Diomedes as we walked towards his chariot, leaving the brother surgeons to retrieve the arrow and examine the body further, then to clean him up making him fit for Agamemnon to see in the morning. 'It seems you were not the only rhapsode on the Rat's murder list. I had no idea when I agreed to keep an eye on you for Odysseus that the profession of rhapsode was such a dangerous one.'

'In my experience, Majesty, it only becomes dangerous when rhapsodes become the repositories of dangerous secrets or the bearers of deadly messages.'

'I know what secrets you know,' said Diomedes pensively as we climbed aboard and the charioteer set the horses in motion. 'But precisely who are they dangerous to?'

'To the High King or his senior, most trusted generals,' I answered. 'Obviously to whichever of them killed the sacred stag and is trying at any cost to avoid risking the lives of his children. But even more now to the High King himself because the wind has stopped and no matter what the real reason for this dead calm may be, the army is beginning to believe it's the hand of the Goddess, and the only way forward is to unmask the guilty man and sacrifice his child.'

'Old ground,' said Diomedes. 'We've gone over it before and I'm convinced. Our next step must turn around the two daggers.' He fell silent, clearly thinking. The chariot rolled back onto the Thebes road and swung right at once, taking us down through the western gate and into Aulis itself.

So I continued, voicing what I assumed his thoughts to be as we followed the main street towards the central square of the Agora. 'We must discover where the jewelled dagger really came from and who set the Rat with his unusual dagger to killing rhapsodes. On the assumption that it could well be the same man. The one who was guilty of killing the stag and the priestess in the first place.'

'But it seems to me,' Diomedes continued, as the chariot came to rest outside the stables where the horses were kept and we stepped down side by side, 'that this murder makes it less likely that the High King himself is guilty. Why would he send his own rhapsode – presumably with a secret message - to Queen Clytemnestra or someone else at his court in Mycenae and then have him murdered almost immediately after he left our camp?'

'Which brings us back to Prince Machaon's original question,' I said. 'If not Agamemnon himself, then who would dare to have the High King's messenger murdered?'

'Hmmm,' said Diomedes. 'We can only find that out if we can track down this man you call the Rat. And off-hand I'd say that was somewhere between unlikely and impossible. One man in an army of fifty thousand…' He looked around himself as though surprised to see where he was. 'Are you planning to stay here in the city tonight?' he asked.

'I was planning on going back aboard *Thalassa*, Majesty,' I answered, my voice, I suspect, showing how depressed I was by the accuracy of his statement. I doubted even King Odysseus would have been able to find the Rat – one man among fifty thousand.

'Then walk with me,' suggested Diomedes, no doubt seeing how crest-fallen I was. 'Pause at my tent for something to eat. Nestor's men should have been out catching some fresh fish but I know the old man was hoping to get hold of a goat or two. It won't be anything like last night's feast but still…' He looked around the square. The afternoon was approaching evening and the stalls were closing down for the night. It would be curfew soon.

We had just set out, side by side again, when Ikaros came hurrying out of the street which led to my father's house. 'There you are!' he said. 'I've been looking for you.'

'At my home, obviously,' I said.

'At your home, aboard *Thalassa*, in Odysseus' tent: everywhere. A wasted afternoon for me – all so that I can return your bag.' He handed it to me as he spoke. 'The High Priestess thanks you and is convinced by your statement that the sacred stag was eaten at Agamemnon's feast last night. She hopes King Odysseus may be able to see more in these things than she could, when he returns. And he's due soon – or so the Oracle says. Any further news about the dead rhapsode?'

'He's with the physicians now,' I said. 'We spent some time there talking to Machaon and his brother. Sophos was their first corpse, apparently; unlikely as that sounds!'

'First among many if Agamemnon gets his way,' added Diomedes.

'Well, that should put your mind at rest, then,' said Ikaros.

'How so?' I asked, failing to follow his reasoning.

'It means I didn't kill the Rat with that slingshot after all. I'd wager he was somewhere there in the sick tents though, if you'd looked. He may not be dead, but he won't be out and about cutting throats for a good long time!'

***

I stopped and turned to the retired hunter, gaping. I could have kicked myself, had I been capable of kicking anything much. Oh, how I missed Odysseus in that moment. There we were, Diomedes and I, discussing the impossibility of tracking down the Rat when we must have spent a good deal of time in the hospital tent within twenty podes foot-lengths of him. Odysseus would never have allowed such a simple oversight! Indeed, I thought ruefully, he would probably have asked Machaon where the man with the bruised temple was being tended and have been directed immediately to the Rat's bedside. Further, I reflected bitterly, Machaon might well have been able to describe the men who brought him in – for Rat would never have been able to make it on his own, judging by the state we left him in. Those men would lead in turn to the leader of the army they were part of. And so we could have deduced the name of the man who killed the stag, who tried to have me murdered and who had asked for Sophos' head!

I turned to Diomedes. 'Majesty,' I said. 'I must return to

Prince Machaon's tent. Ikaros is right, the Rat might well be there. I may have the chance to talk to him; to ask some questions and hope to do so safely, surrounded by the physicians' helpers and the other patients. I might even hope for a truthful reply!'

'I will accompany you,' decided the young king. 'I gave my word to Odysseus to watch out for you.'

'And I'll come too,' said Ikaros. 'I'm already involved in this up to my neck and I really want to find out what in the names of all the gods is actually going on!'

The three of us set off at as rapid a pace as I could manage. We went out through the southern gate just as the guards were assembling to close it at curfew. Oddly the sun seemed to set later out on the slopes where the tents were pitched than it did in the valley where the city sat. We used the last of the light as the sun westered behind the tree-lined ridges of the Groves of Artemis, and arrived at the physicians' tents just as twilight was closing down. As there was in Aulis, so there seemed to be a sort of curfew here. The helpers were scarcer. Machaon had gone – no doubt invited to another of Agamemnon's feasts. His brother was just getting ready to leave as well, but he accorded Diomedes more courtesy than he might have exercised, perhaps, on Ikaros and myself had we not been accompanied by a king. 'Welcome back, King Diomedes,' he said. 'If you're looking for more information about poor Sophos you have arrived too soon. We will try to free the arrow and do the further assessment in the morning. He is packed away for now.'

'It's not that…' Diomedes explained our new mission.

'Yes,' said Podialirius. 'Now you mention it, I remember a man being brought in with just such a headwound as you are describing. One of the assistants saw who brought him to us. I never saw them; only the patient they had brought.'

'A scrawny, rat-faced man,' I added, making a mental note to see whether I could find the assistant Podialirius referred to should the Rat prove less than helpful.

'That's right,' said Podialirius.

'Can you tell us where he is?' I asked.

'I can do better than that,' said Podialirius. 'I can take you to him.' The physician led the way out of the large tent, pausing at a table by the doorway to light a lamp which he took to light our way into the shadows of the tent a few doors down. As with most of the tents, there was no flooring – not even the rugs that the kings and princes tended to use. But rather than have his patients sleep on the ground, Podialirius had arranged for makeshift beds to be made with linen bags stuffed with straw and pine-needles for mattresses. The Rat was lying on one of these, covered with his cloak. The bruise on his left temple seemed to have spread across much of his left profile. He appeared to be in a deep sleep, but when Podialirius held the lamp close to him he stirred. He blinked. His eyes opened. The left one was bloodshot, the lids slightly swollen. The right one was clear, its pupil a sort of dirty brown. I saw it focus on the lamp flame, then on Podialirius who was holding the lamp, on Diomedes, Ikaros and finally on me. All without the slightest flicker of recognition.

'He seems to have no memory,' said Podialirius quietly, speaking as though Rat wasn't there at all. 'That is why I was keen to bring some people he might recognise to his bedside. A familiar face might stir some memories. What did you say his name is?'

'Arouraios,' I answered. 'Rat.'

'Hello Arouraios,' said the physician. 'Do you remember me?'

Rat looked at him blankly. He might as well have been speaking Hittite, Egyptian or Babylonian.

'These men, Arouraios. They say they know you. Do you recognise them?'

Still no reaction. I reached into my bag and pulled out the gaudy dagger. He didn't even blink. Finally I pulled his own serrated blade out and held it in the light.

Nothing.

'I have come across this before with head wounds,' said Podialirius. 'He remembers nothing and no-one.'

'Will his memory return?' I asked, putting the daggers away, looking down on the bruised, blank countenance with disappointment and frustration.

'Almost certainly. But I'm afraid I cannot tell you when it will do so – or indeed, how much of it will actually be there when it does.'

iii

The servant who saw the Rat's arrival had gone for the night. Diomedes and I decided to come back in the morning, therefore, and see whether Rat's memory had begun to return or whether the man who received him could describe – perhaps even identify – the men who brought him in. Ikaros wavered indecisively. On the one hand he really ought to be getting back to the Temple of Artemis. On the other hand, he was keen to accompany the king and me in the morning. It was Diomedes' offer of dinner that decided the matter. When the three of us arrived at Diomedes' tent and the open space it shared with Nestor's, the elderly king of Pylos was busily overseeing the meal's preparation himself, telling his cook a lengthy story about a meal he and his fellow Argonaut Admetus, King of Pherae, had prepared for Jason and Medea on the way back from Colchis. 'Of course, that was a boar and all we have here is a goat, but the technique is the same. A glaze of honey mixed with olive oil…'

Diomedes interrupted the old king courteously but firmly – in my experience the only way to get a word in – and explained he had brought two guests to the modest feast. Nestor knew me; he and I had been involved together in Odysseus' search for Achilles at Phthia and on Skyros. But he had not met Ikaros. Many kings – Palamedes and Aias for example – would have been insulted to find a rhapsode and a temple servant as guests but Nestor's open heart and firm belief in xenia, the duty of hospitality, were amongst his greatest strengths. 'The Temple of Artemis?' he said to Ikaros as soon as Diomedes introduced him. 'That's odd. I was just describing a meal I cooked with King Admetus of Pherae and of course, as I'm sure you know, Admetus and Artemis had the most terrible falling-out over his failure to sacrifice to her at his wedding. So when he entered the bridal chamber expecting to find his lovely new wife Alcestis, he found masses of deadly snakes instead! Huge vipers, mostly grey with black markings, some of them as long as my leg! Terrible! It took the direct intervention of Apollo to sort everything out. I'll tell you the full story precisely as Admetus told it to me while we eat.' He turned to his attendants. 'Someone bring more wine…'

Ikaros and I walked less than steadily back to *Thalassa* a good deal later, our bellies full of honeyed goat, our heads fuddled with the wine that accompanied the old king's lengthy reminiscence and our minds filled with pictures of grey-bodied, black-marked vipers as long as our legs who obeyed the whims of the easily infuriated Goddess. Fortunately, we didn't meet any of Artemis' fearsome pets and made it back to *Thalassa* where we were able to make ourselves makeshift beds on the deck by the light of the waning moon. I fell into one of the deepest sleeps I can remember. Ikaros said later that he actually thought I had died in the night for I lay there more like a corpse than a sleeper.

An unnaturally bright morning found us with sore heads and dry throats but fresh-baked emmer-bread, honey and cold spring water went a long way towards restoring us. Then, we set off for Machaon's tent to see whether the Rat's memory was beginning to return. Once again I was carrying my leather bag, but this time I had left the skull and the foreleg in acting-Captain Eurylocus' safe keeping. All the satchel now contained were the knives and the broken arrow.

We paused at Diomedes' tent to find the young king up, but Nestor unusually still asleep. So, once more the three of us set out side by side. We found Machaon immediately when we arrived and that was enough to distract us from our planned mission. For he was performing the most delicate of operations, trying to cut the arrow free of Sophos' naked chest. He had several helpers working alongside him. There were bowls of water, various implements, linen cloths and surprisingly little blood – given that the physician had made a considerable incision between the ribs where the arrow was lodged and was trying to work it free with both his huge fingers and some sort of gripping implement.

'I had to snap the shaft,' he told us as he worked. 'There was no other way to remove the poor man's clothing. But I have kept the flight-end safe for you and I have every hope that the arrowhead will soon join it so that you can compare the pair of them. I have examined the body fully now that I have had it stripped and it is clear to me that our conversation yesterday covered all the important points. The arrow knocked him off his horse but did not kill him at once. He was still alive and lying on his back when his throat was cut. Someone of considerable strength held his head still while his companion first slit and then sawed at the gullet, trying to remove the head. Everything about the corpse from the wound in the throat and the arrow in his side to the bruising on his left knee, hip, elbow, arm and shoulder bears this out.'

\*\*\*

'It looks as though he didn't fight back if those are the only marks on him,' I said. 'Surely there would have been bruises at least if he was held down while trying to escape. On his shoulders or his arms, perhaps.'

'And that would have left some sign at the spot on the roadside where he died,' added Ikaros. 'But there was nothing apart from footprints and the track of the body being pulled away. Only the blood.'

'Yes. He was, perhaps, lucky: he seems to have been unconscious at the end. There is a swelling on the back of his skull I assumed he sustained in the fall from his horse but he might have been clubbed into the bargain; perhaps when his attackers realised he was not quite dead yet. A good point. I will explain to the High King when he arrives that Sophos was unconscious at the end. It might make things easier for him. This will come as quite a shock, I'm afraid. Sophos was a valued servant and something of a confidante I understand.'

'Is the High King coming now?' I asked, thinking back to Diomedes' warning. Agamemnon was one enemy I could well do without, always assuming he wasn't after my head already.

'I have sent Podialirius to request his presence but neither one has returned as yet. If experience is anything to go by, Agamemnon will take his time; he does not react swiftly to such requests, even from other monarchs. Yet another way of emphasising his standing and importance. He is after all the *Spudeos* Basileus, the *High* King.'

'In the mean-time,' said Diomedes, 'Podialirius told us that one of your servants tending the hurt and wounded saw who brought the Rat in yesterday. Do you know which man that was?'

'No, I'm afraid not. You'll have to wait for Podialirius to return and ask him.'

'While we're waiting,' I said, 'may we go and see whether the Rat remembers any more than he did when we talked to him yesterday?'

'Of course. Do you know where he is?'

'We do,' said Diomedes, and led the way out of Machaon's tent. As I followed Diomedes, I could feel my breath shorten and my heart speed up in anticipation. I really hoped that the Rat would tell us who had tasked him with the murders he had undertaken – in my case with limited success. Or, failing that, we would find the servant who accepted him into the facility and get a description of the men who brought him in. What a coup it would be, I thought, if King Odysseus returned – as he was bound to do at almost any moment – to find that I had managed to unmask the priestess' killer and

111

the rhapsode's murderer without him!

The tent where the Rat was being tended was silent. Half a dozen figures lay, raised a handsbreadth off the ground by the straw-stuffed mattresses, covered in a variety of cloaks which were clearly serving a makeshift blankets. I shook my head in mild surprise – I hadn't realised there were that many last night. But they had all been hidden in shadows of course while we were concentrating on the puddle of brightness from Podialirius' lamp. There was no-one tending them but then again none of them were demanding attention either. We moved amongst them as silently as possible, searching for the Rat's bruised face. He was further from the entrance than I remembered but I eventually found him, covered to the chin by his threadbare cloak, and signalled to the others. Still staying quiet, we gathered round his bed. 'He seems to be sleeping soundly,' whispered Diomedes. 'It's almost a pity to wake him.'

'I hesitate to disagree, Majesty,' said Ikaros. 'But the murderous little bastard doesn't deserve any courtesy from us!' He leaned down and took the Rat by his shoulder, shaking him vigorously immediately he did so.'

'Shhh!' said somebody. I glanced up, wondering who it could be. The sound seemed to be coming from behind us. Perhaps an attendant had returned unnoticed.

'SHHHHH!' said the mysterious voice again. But there was no-one else there.

'Look out!' shouted Ikaros. He jumped back, cannoned into me and nearly sent me sprawling. His elbow slammed into my temple. Among the flashes of light that danced round the edge of my damaged vision, I saw Diomedes leaping back as well. The cloak covering the Rat heaved with a strange, inhuman life of its own, as though the murderer's scrawny body was being transformed into something sinisterly serpentine.

Then the cloak slipped aside and the sinuous form of a viper slithered down onto the ground. Grey-bodied, black-marked and every bit as long as our legs.

iv

'This is most unusual,' said Machaon looking down at the Rat's black and swollen face. 'Did anyone see where the snake went?' He looked up across the table where Sophos had lain earlier. The rhapsode was stretched out on a straw-stuffed mattress, covered from the shoulders down with a linen sheet, awaiting a visit from his king. Both halves of the arrow were in my satchel ready for a detailed comparison with the one that had killed the priestess and the stag, though at first glance they seemed to be very different from each-other. The physician's brother had returned without Agamemnon and was now out with as many helpers as could be spared, searching for the snake and any others that might be nearby.

'No, Majesty,' I said. 'It vanished while we were checking to see whether anyone else in the tent had been bitten.'

'And had they?'

'No.'

'Podialirius will tell us whether anyone in the other tents was also poisoned and whether there's anything else nearby that looks dangerous. In the mean-time, this man has been bitten several times as you can see. All the bite-marks are in the throat area which is why it is so terribly swollen. The first or second must have killed him. An aspis you said...'

'Grey and black and as long as my leg, maybe longer.' I repeated what I had already told his brother.

'He must have tried to fight it off,' said Ikaros. 'I certainly would have.'

'But why was it there in the first place?' wondered Diomedes.

'Cold night, warm body just above the ground; an excellent resting-place,' said Machaon. 'Warm to begin with, anyway. It's cold now.'

'And that's probably why the creature was so sluggish

when we found it,' said Ikaros.

'Lucky for us it was,' I said, nodding my agreement.

'Well,' said Diomedes, pulling us back to our mission. 'We've wasted our time coming here. He's not going to tell us anything now.'

'I don't know, Majesty,' I said. 'Perhaps if we find the servant who took him in and can track whoever brought him in the first place...'

But no sooner had I finished speaking than events took an unexpected turn. Podialirius pushed through the tent-flap and paused holding it open. Outside there was a small group of men I did not recognise. 'You see?' Podialirius was saying. 'Your friend died in the night, bitten by an asp. The leader of the little group, who bore a striking resemblance to the man the bear crushed, stepped respectfully into the tent, head bowed, face set like stone. He was so massive and hairy that he might well have passed for a bear himself – a likeness emphasised by the shaggy skin garment he was wearing. He reached out a hesitant hand and felt the Rat's stone-cold forehead. 'He was our companion, Majesty. May we take him and oversee his funeral?'

Machaon looked at the man, frowning. 'Wait outside,' he said abruptly. 'You may have him when I've finished with him.' He waved the Bear away. The soldier turned obediently and joined his associates just beyond the doorway. Podialirius let the leather curtain fall behind him.

'Well,' said Ikaros. 'Not such a waste of time after all, begging your pardon for disagreeing, Majesty.'

'Even if those are not the men who brought him in, the fact they're here to take him away will do just as well,' said Diomedes with a nod of agreement.

'What approach would be the best, I wonder?' I said. 'Should we just go out and question them – or should we wait until Prince Machaon releases the body and then follow them to see where they take it?'

'Maybe a bit of both, what do you think?' suggested Ikaros.

'You go and question them while I sneak out the back and get ready to follow them when they take the body.'

'Good idea,' said Diomedes decisively. 'As long as Machaon and Podialirius here are in agreement.'

'Of course,' said Machaon. 'That's fine with us.'

He had hardly finished speaking before Diomedes was out of the tent and confronting the Bear. I stood just behind him, trying my best to look invisible. These were the friends and colleagues of a man who had tried to kill me twice, after all. Any one of them might be tasked with finishing his work.

'You, there!' said Diomedes. 'You know who I am?' He drew himself up to his full height and glared down his nose in a fine impersonation of Palamedes.

'Yes, Majesty,' said the Bear, his tone ingratiating, almost grovelling. Diomedes took this as a matter of course – I was less convinced but there was nothing I could do to share my doubts 'You are King Diomedes of Argos,' said the Bear.

'Good. In that case you know how dangerous it would be if you were to lie to me.'

'Yes, Majesty. I would never dream of doing such a thing.' The group behind him growled in gruff agreement, as unconvincing as the Bear's humility.

'Whose army are you with?' demanded King Diomedes.

'We serve with Aias, King of the Locrians, Majesty,' came the unhesitating answer.

\*\*\*

'That was easy enough,' said Diomedes as we watched the Bear and his companions take the Rat's body out of Machaon's tent, followed by the brother physicians off about their work and leaving the pair of us alone. 'But what do we do with the information?'

'Aias,' I said. 'Palamedes' companion in the investigation of the priestess' death. I wonder whether Palamedes asked for his help – or whether Aias offered it.'

'The difference being…'

'It might be that Palamedes was commissioned, as

Odysseus suspected, to frustrate the aims of the enquiry and ensure that whoever was found guilty could in no way reflect on the High King or indeed his high command. He could have done this well enough without Aias' assistance, for, despite his faults he is massively creative and fearsomely intelligent. If he did ask for help, however, then it might well have been that there was something in the enquiry that even he could not understand or handle on his own.'

'Unlikely though that sounds,' said Diomedes pensively. 'Though, now I think of it, it might have been something that required action rather than thought; something that needed throats cut or backs stabbed rather than arguments won or problems reasoned out.'

'However,' I continued, 'if Aias pushed his way into the enquiry so to speak, then he must have an agenda that goes further than simply helping his friend by supplying some ruthless killers. An agenda, seemingly, that involves dead rhapsodes. But even then, there's something more. Something at the back of my mind that I cannot quite put my finger on…'

'That,' said Diomedes, 'will be the element that Odysseus will work out for you as soon as he returns.'

That was as far as our discussion had reached before the tent flap was raised once more and Machaon ushered two of his helpers into the tent. They almost ran to the linen-draped Sophos and one took his shoulders while the other took his ankles and with a practised motion they swung him back up onto Machaon's table, despite his pendant arms and the strange behaviour of his half-severed head. Machaon fussed about the body at once, tucking in the limbs, straightening the linen sheet and settling the head so that the gape of the throat was mostly closed. No sooner had he done this than Podialirius also returned, but this time in elevated company. The High King was dressed in a himation of Tyrian purple with gilded edges. His belt and sandals were of the finest leather, studded and fastened with gold. Even though he wore no head dress, everything about him seemed to shout *I am the Spudeos Basileus High King here; even the gods bow down to me.* Behind him stood a squad of attendants, held back by a curt gesture as he came onwards alone.

'Well?' snapped Agamemnon as he stooped for an instant to enter the tent then drew himself up to his full, regal height, 'what is it you want me to see? Show it to me and be quick about it I haven't much time…'

Machaon stepped back, revealing Sophos on the table. 'This is what we wanted to show you, Spudeos Basileus.'

High King Agamemnon glanced at the body and was actually in the act of shrugging dismissively when he stopped. An expression of shock came onto his face; surprise so profound that it bordered on horror. 'Sophos,' he said, his voice ragged, as though he had been screaming for a long time before he spoke. 'How could it be Sophos?' the question was almost a whisper. He swung round passing from consternation to outrage in a heartbeat. 'Who has dared do this?' he snarled.

We all looked at him silently because of course none of us knew the answer he was seeking, and *"the Rat, who serves Aias of Locris did it"* was not going to get us anywhere and might even get us killed.

The High King used the silence to gain some measure of control over himself. 'Where was he found?' he asked, his voice steadier.

Diomedes told him, 'By the road to Thebes, in the Groves of Artemis there.'

'When was he found?'

Again, Diomedes told him. But then he added, 'It seems certain he had been lying there for some time. He was killed while travelling towards Thebes, almost certainly soon after you sent him.'

'Going towards Thebes,' echoed Agamemnon. 'Going *towards* Thebes. Not coming back from Thebes?'

'No, Spudeos Basileus,' said Diomedes. 'We have been to

the place and saw the body there before we brought it back here. There is no doubt. He was going towards Thebes when he was murdered.'

'This can't be,' croaked Agamemnon. '*This can't be*!' he was raging again, almost completely out of control.

When a broad hand lifted the leather curtain to reveal Odysseus' most trusted oarsman and servant Elpenor; the man who had led the king's entourage on the journey to Ithaka. And now, clearly, back from Ithaka. 'Spudeos Basileus,' he said to Agamemnon, 'I have been sent on ahead by King Odysseus to bring great news! My King is in company with Queen Clytemnestra, Prince Orestes, Princess Iphigenia and their attendants. They met when they stayed overnight in Thebes. Now they have all left Thebes together, and will be here soon. The Queen has asked me to request that you begin preparations for the wedding ceremony and the great feasts that must accompany it at once!' He dropped the curtain as he turned and walked away.


v

High King Agamemnon strode out of the tent in silence, his face as white as the marble of Mount Pentelicus. His attendants who had been waiting outside fell in around him – and that was just as well because it seemed for a moment that they would need to hold him up. He paused for a moment, spitting orders. Several attendants sped away, running in all directions through the camp. Then the High King was in motion once again. As we watched him walk away, Diomedes said, 'A wedding, eh? I wonder who's getting married.'

'Princess Iphigenia, clearly,' said Machaon. 'But as to who she's marrying, your guess is as good as mine!'

'Surely it shouldn't be too hard to work out,' I said, buoyed up by the promise of my captain's imminent return. 'It has to be a king or a prince at least. And how many are suitable, available and unmarried? Most of them are either married already, too old or both. Amongst the younger generation, who do we have? Palamedes and Aias for a start. Leitus of Boeotia, Prince Ajax isn't married yet…'

'I'm just married to my lovely Aegialia,' remember, warned Diomedes. 'So don't get carried away and put me on your wedding-list!'

'Thalpius of Elis,' I persisted.

'And the vast majority of the others were suitors for Helen's hand alongside Meneleus,' said Diomedes. 'They're all from the same generation as Iphegenia's father therefore, and far too old, though King Nireus of Syme is wearing outstandingly well. And they're all married!'

'Well, I concluded, 'let's hope it's not Palamedes or Aias. I wouldn't wish either of them on the daughter of my greatest enemy!'

We left Machaon's tent but I hesitated almost at once. Odysseus was going to arrive soon. Perhaps I should wait at his tent. Then I remembered that much of what I wished to show him was aboard *Thalassa*, so I would have to go via the ship, no-matter what my final destination. Then it struck me that Elpenor's message would put a whole new aspect onto the investigation in any case. Would Odysseus want to become involved in something as sordid as the murders I had been investigating when the festivities of a royal wedding were just about to start?

'Make up your mind, lad,' said Diomedes. 'Where do you want to go?'

'I want to see King Odysseus arriving,' I said – or rather blurted.

'Well, that's easily done,' said the young king. 'He's escorting Queen Clytemnestra and the children. He'll be going to see them safely to High King Agamemnon's tent.'

So as Diomedes went directly to his own tent to give Nestor the news – if he didn't already know it - I went down to *Thalassa* as quickly as I was able and hauled myself aboard. 'The captain's back!' I called to acting-Captain Eurylocus as

I grabbed the shattered foreleg and the skull, stuffing them into my bag beside the daggers and the arrows, excitement overcoming the second thoughts I had already started to entertain about the appropriateness of bringing such violent matters to a wedding festival. 'He's accompanying Queen Clytemnestra. Apparently Princess Iphigenia is getting married to one of the suitable young kings or princes.'

'Perhaps the High King's hoping that such an auspicious occasion will make the Goddess change her mind and let the wind loose,' said Eurylocus sceptically. 'As long as he doesn't mess it up like King Admetus did in the stories old King Nestor likes to tell. I hear there have been vipers loose in the camp today already.'

'A wedding ceremony to appease Artemis. That hadn't occurred to me,' I said, dismissing the snake story with a shrug. 'Do you think there's any chance…' I stopped because I realised I was asking the wrong man. I ought to be asking Ikaros: he'd have a good idea of what the High Priestess and the Oracle would think of the notion – or rather what they thought the Goddess would think of it. Then something struck me: I hadn't actually seen Ikaros since the Bear and his companions had carried the Rat's body off, no doubt to be disposed of in whatever ritual his master King Aias dictated. He must have followed them to the Locrian camp, I supposed, and would have no idea that matters had changed in his absence. However, I had no intention of going to try and find him. I was going to get to Agamemnon's tent with all possible dispatch in case Odysseus arrived before I got there. Though to be fair I was also interested to see Queen Clytemnestra and Princess Iphigenia, though the maiden would probably be veiled. Clytemnestra was sister to the kidnapped Helen, Queen of Sparta and wife to Menelaus. Helen was supposed to be the most beautiful woman alive, and her sister was hardly less lovely. As far as I had heard, the only real difference was that Helen had blonde hair and blue eyes while Clytemnestra was dark. Their characters were different too by all accounts: Helen was cheerfully sunny but fatally biddable; Clytemnestra had an unbreakable will and a memory for slights and insults rivalled only by that of the Goddess Artemis herself. But rumour had it that the budding beauty of Agamemnon's favourite daughter Iphigenia bid fair to outdo both her mother and her aunt in time and rival even the exquisite Aphrodite, Goddess of Love and Beauty.

As I hurried towards Agamemnon's tent, my head full of these thoughts, Ikaros appeared at my side. 'Once I heard the news,' he said companionably as though we had already been conversing for some time, 'I knew I'd find you somewhere between *Thalassa* and the High King's tent. Do you know when Odysseus is due to arrive?'

'No,' I said. 'But I'm surprised that the news actually reached you and that you made it here so quickly. The Locrian camp is one of the outer ones. Did you run?'

'No,' said Ikaros. 'I didn't need to. The Bear and his little funeral party didn't go anywhere near Aias's camp. They took the Rat straight to King Menelaus.'

***

The only reason I did not stop and gape at him was my fear that I might miss Odysseus' arrival if I did so. 'Menelaus,' I said. 'But why would the High King's brother have anything to do with a creature like the Rat?'

'Only one reason I can think of,' answered Ikaros cheerfully. 'King Menelaus must have employed him!'

'To kill poor Sophos and stop the message he was carrying getting to Mycenae,' I reasoned, slowing my pace as I tried to work things through. 'But why would Menelaus *want* to kill the rhapsode and stop the message? Why interfere with the High King's plans?'

'Perhaps because the High King's plans somehow interfere with his brother's plans or wishes,' said Ikaros.

'Well, I'd be surprised if that were the case!' I countered. 'Menelaus simply wants to get to Troy as soon as possible, rescue his beautiful wife from Prince Paris and take her home to Sparta. That seems to be all there is. All this talk of sacking the city, amassing mountains of loot, and getting our fill of slaughter and rapine seems to be coming from Agamemnon and his closest associates.'

'It's all to motivate the troops,' said Ikaros. 'they need good reasons to stick with his plan. Menelaus doesn't want to plunder anywhere. He probably wouldn't want to kill Prince Paris if it wasn't a matter of honour. All he wants is Helen. Home.'

'True,' I said. 'So, what in Agamemnon's plans could be running counter to such a simple desire?'

'Well, as we've just found out, the High King plans to keep us all here – whether the wind returns or not – so that he can marry Princess Iphigenia off to one of the thoroughly eligible royal bachelors assembled in and around the camp. That is bound to slow things down with regard to Helen's rescue.'

'Unless, as Odysseus' acting captain Eurylocus suggested,' I said, 'that the wedding is itself a ploy to distract the Goddess. Or even to make her forget her outrage at the death of the sacred stag and the priestess and release the west wind after all.'

Ikaros gave a bark of cynical laughter. 'If that's his plan, he should just forget it. The only thing that will appease the Goddess is the sacrifice of a child sired by the man who fired that fatal arrow. Until that happens, the thousand ships and fifty thousand men are stuck here and going nowhere unless they decide to go home.'

'And if that happens it spells humiliation and ruin for both of the sons of Atreus,' I said. 'So Agamemnon and Menelaus have the same long term goal. Get to Troy, get into the city, get back home with either a massive fortune or a flighty wife – depending on which brother you are. Whatever is causing disagreement between them must be more immediate in nature.'

'Well,' said Ikaros, 'you must admit the High King has not

been particularly active in the unmasking of the guilty man – no matter what his reasons! If he'd been serious about pleasing the High Priestess and appeasing the Goddess, he would never have sent King Odysseus away. He needs to take decisive action but he's playing politics instead. If I was Menelaus, married to the most beautiful mortal alive and some Trojan princeling was bedding my wife nightly somewhere in his father's citadel, I'd be verging on madness with rage at my brother sitting on his hands like this, especially when he'd promised to do all he could to help get her back!'

'So,' I said, as the High King's tent came into sight and we could see the two brothers Menelaus and Agamemnon standing in front of it, both dressed in purple and armed in gold, waiting magnificently for the Queen's arrival, 'it seems that we have to work on the assumption that, in spite of their show of unity, the two brothers are actually working against each-other.'

'And,' added Ikaros as the parade of wagons, pack-animals and servants or slaves on foot led by King Odysseus and Queen Clytemnestra side by side in their chariots appeared, 'it looks as though Palamedes has been working for Agamemnon…'

'While Aias and his murderers are really Menelaus' men,' I said.

## 6 - The Return of the King

i

At first, Queen Clytemnestra's arrival appeared to lighten the mood in the vast Achaean camp. The sons of Atreus, her husband and his brother, were both apparently overjoyed to see Clytemnestra, Iphigenia and little Orestes who, unlike his sisters Electra and Laodike, was too young to be left behind in the royal citadel of Mycenae. It was only when I eventually got to talk to Odysseus that the first shadows of suspicion that all was not well began to gather.

At first glance Odysseus himself appeared to be as elated as everyone else at the promise of a royal wedding and the associated festivities which would, at the very least, fill up the next few days if they too proved to be windless. He only let his guard down later, in his tent, long before I had an opportunity to discuss with him the things that I had found out so far. It was not surprising, of course, that my captain's seeming cheerfulness in company should mask a deeper sadness which only revealed itself in more private moments. After all, he had just parted once again from his own beloved Queen Penelope and his son Prince Telemachus. He had no idea when or if he would see them again because he suspected that many weary years and dangerous campaigns might well stand between his recent parting and his eventual return. And to rub salt in the wound, here was Agamemnon calling his wife and son to-be with him while he solemnised his beloved daughter's marriage. But the wedding itself was the first aspect which called a dark thought to my captain's lips.

'Perhaps,' said Odysseus as he sat in his tent soon after his arrival while the crewmen who had accompanied him sent the chariot back to its stable in Aulis, brought various items in and marked others for transport to *Thalassa*. One of his servants washed his travel-stained feet and legs while he rubbed the side of his thigh, seemingly lost in dream as he continued, 'it is the thought that any father has when looking on the loveliest of his daughters – that he is soon to lose her to marriage and another man. No matter how much she loves him, the day will come when she loves another man more. This is the dreadful moment at which the High King seems to have arrived. Perhaps that explains the shadows of sorrow and desperation I seem to see beneath Agamemnon's smile. It is selfish, I know, but there are times I thank the Gods that I have fathered a son. In the mean-time,' he continued, rousing himself, 'I have called you here because there are several things I need to discuss with you. The first and most important is that Sophos, the High King's rhapsode has been killed.'

'I know this, Captain. I have been looking...'

'And *therefore*,' Odysseus rode over my enthusiastic reply with a firmness that I attributed to his exhaustion and sadness, 'the High King is currently without the usual entertainment at his feasts. The first of which is being prepared as we speak. He requires, in consequence, that you wait on him as soon as possible to discuss which of your songs would be best suited to the happy occasion. You will perform it for his guests tonight.'

Those words stopped me in my tracks and emptied my mind of everything I had been planning to discuss. 'I had better go at once,' I said.

'Yes, you had,' said Odysseus wearily. He stopped massaging the scar that ran up the outside of his thigh – something he only did when he was extremely tired - and waved me away. He had been given that scar by a huge boar during a hunt on Mount Parnassus with his grandfather Autolycus in his youth, much to the horror of King Laertes his father and Queen Anticlea his mother. He had been very lucky to survive. There were dangers in being a father to boys as well as to girls, I thought.

I was no sooner outside his tent than I realised that I could not, in fact, obey the High King's summons immediately. The leather bag which currently hung from my shoulder contained the things I wished to show my captain – two daggers, two arrows which appeared to be nothing alike, a skull and a shattered shank. The bag I needed, the one that contained my lyre, was on *Thalassa*. I turned, therefore and began to run as fast as I could down the hillside towards the shore. The distance was not great – Odysseus liked to pitch his tent where he could see his vessel, even in the distance. I was running along the shore towards the beached ship, therefore, when something else distracted me. I slowed to a walk, frowning. My adventures as I escaped the Rat immediately after his companion had been crushed by the bear had taken me through the Myrmidons' camp. Their tents were beyond the point where *Thalassa* lay but they were still easily visible, as were the black ships drawn up on the sand opposite them and it was what was going on here that engaged my attention.

The entire Myrmidon army was astir. It seemed that all two thousand five hundred of them were vacating their tents, pulling on their armour, grabbing their spears and shields as they lined up, rank after rank, along the firm grassy area behind the dunes. Fascinated and not a little surprised, I ran past *Thalassa*, looking for a familiar face among the regimented lines. As fortune would have it, I saw Eudorus, one of the five commanders who ranked immediately below Achilles and Patroclus. I had met him when I visited Phthia and he recognised me. The five hundred soldiers of his command had just formed up in front of him and they were all awaiting their leader's next command. 'General,' I called. 'What is going on?'

\*\*\*

'Orders,' answered General Eudorus with a philosophical shrug.

'But what is it that you're being ordered to do?' I asked.

126

'We're off on a forced march,' he said tersely. 'To test the men and sharpen up any slackness. Here to Marathon. Leaving now. Armoured and fully armed. Prince Achilles and Patroclus in the lead. On foot like the rest of us. At a run to begin with.'

'Marathon is, what, twelve leagues distant,' I calculated. 'Nothing much in the way of roads and some really mountainous sections. Challenging stuff.'

'Right. We're Myrmidons. Twelve leagues is hardly any distance at all. Marching us that far along the beach would be a waste of our time, even in this heat and even if we ran part of the way. But the terrain to the south of here is what makes it challenging, especially as we'll have to go round or climb over Mount Parthina. We'll be at Marathon by nightfall though, no matter what. We'll sleep out on the plain, forage what we can, pretend we're on the Troad looking up at the walls of Troy, then wait for further orders.'

No sooner had he finished speaking than the order to move out came. The ranks of soldiers facing eastwards towards the sea swung round, moving as though they were all one man, and began to run southwards, General Eudorus at their side. Black armour gleaming, arm-guards and greaves flashing, shields on one shoulder, spears on the other, swords slapping against thighs, helmet plumes flirting like black mares' tails in the still, sultry air. My mind filled with pleasurable thoughts about what would happen to the murderous Trojan thieves who had robbed and crippled me on the dockside there when the Myrmidons got hold of them. I turned and walked back to *Thalassa*. As quickly as I could, I climbed aboard, swapped one bag for another and returned to the beach. I was just setting off for the High King's tent when a frog-faced man I recognised as one of the royal servants came puffing down to the sand only to stop, frowning with confusion.

'What's the matter?' I asked.

'I've been told to deliver a message,' he said.

'From whom to whom?'

'From the High King. He sends an invitation for Princes Achilles and Patroclus to attend his feast of welcome for Queen Clytemnestra, Prince Orestes and Princess Iphigenia tonight,' he explained.

'Too late,' I told him. 'Achilles and the Myrmidons have left on a forced march to Marathon. They won't be back for two days, maybe three.'

The royal servant and I walked back towards the High King's tent companionably enough. 'There's going to be a big feast tonight,' I observed. 'I have to sing a song suitable for a wedding at it.'

'To welcome the queen and the princess, yes, though none of us has any idea who the prospective bridegroom is. It's some kind of secret, apparently. Chief Steward Oikonomos has everyone running around like lunatics. I believe the High King has been taken by surprise.'

'What, that the queen arrived so soon?' I wondered.

'That she's arrived at all,' he said. 'Oikonomos says he doesn't think the High King knew she was coming and certainly not on a mission like this! Agamemnon is usually so well-organised. Plenty of planning ahead with detailed warnings for Oikonomos and the rest of us. Not this time! We're scouring everywhere, looking for almost everything! Oikonomos says it's a pity we didn't keep that stag back. It could have hung for a few more days – probably have improved the flavour. But the High King was keen for it to be used so it's gone and that's that. Poor Oikonomos is in the agora in Aulis at the moment. There are traders there who will have made their fortune, I can tell you!'

*Father amongst them, I hope*, I thought. 'But surely,' I said, 'the Queen would never have brought the Princess here without being told to by the High King. Especially as she's expecting there to be a wedding!'

The servant shrugged. 'Perhaps the High King sent her a message then changed his mind and sent another message telling her not to come…'

'And then for some reason,' I said, 'the second message never got through!'

ii

I was still wrestling with the ramifications of that thought when the servant and I arrived at the High King's tent. The whole place seemed to be the centre of a great whirl of activity. Chief Steward Oikonomos and his assistants had just returned from the market in Aulis, pulling carts laden with the skinned carcases of lambs and kids. Anything larger, the size of the stag, for example, would never be cooked in time for tonight's festivities. Even a modest boar or a sizeable ram would have taken most of the day and there was no time for anything bigger than the animals they had brought and the fish in the cart behind them. Slaves and servants were dashing in and out of the front entrance with the focused energy of men bailing a sinking ship. But that was only the half of it. To the rear of the tent, the engineers of Agamemnon's Mycenaean army were extending the domestic sections, fighting to add rooms, ablutions and whatever else was needed, as Queen Clytemnestra's attendants came and went as busily as the High King's cooks and stewards.

I followed the messenger into Oikonomos' areas like a soldier plunging onto a battlefield. The chief steward was at the centre of the activity in the megaron, deciding which carcases should go where around the fire-pit, carefully committing the flesh before the fish. At the same time, he had one eye on the preparation of the tables for the High King the Queen and their royal guests. The scale and mood were very different from last time – as was the atmosphere of near panic which, I hoped, would be replaced by the calm of a placid mountain lake by the time my song was called for. My companion approached the chief steward and waited to be noticed. I did likewise, standing immediately behind him.

'Well?' snapped the beleaguered Oikonomos at last.

'Prince Achilles and Prince Patroclus will not be attending. They have taken the Myrmidons…'

'Taken the Myrmidons? Taken them where in Ares' name?' snarled the harassed steward.

'Taken them on a forced march to Marathon,' I said as the messenger gaped silently, looking even more like a frog, rendered wordless by his superior's anger. 'General Eudorus told me as they left – just before your messenger arrived.'

'And who…' began Oikonomos. But then he recognised me. 'Ah, Odysseus' rhapsode. I hope King Odysseus at least will be gracing us…'

'He will,' I answered. 'But he told me the High King wished to discuss which song I should sing tonight as Sophus can no longer perform.'

'Yes. Poor Sophus. A tragedy and a terrible crime. Perhaps King Odysseus can look into that as well as into the matter of the sacred stag now he has returned. Prince Palamedes doesn't seem to have made much progress. But Prince Achilles has gone to Marathon, you say? Perhaps you had better not break that news to the High King. He seems to be under quite enough pressure today what with one thing and another. Leave the news about Achilles to me. He said I should send you straight to him as soon as you arrived, and I pray to the muses that your song meets with his approval! You!' he pointed at the servant who was still waiting open-mouthed to be dismissed. 'Take the rhapsode to the High King. He is in the propylon beside the temple talking with his brother.'

I followed the servant through the bustling megaron and out at the back into the private areas. Here there was a small open courtyard leading straight ahead into the High King's personal chambers – now being swiftly augmented to contain the queen with her baby son, Princess Iphigenia and their retunes. These extended right up to the main structure of the megaron on my left but opening off the courtyard on my right there was a temple, fronted, as was traditional by a propylon entrance area where those about to enter the sacred space could pause, arrange their thoughts and remove their footwear if necessary. The High King and his brother were in this area, face to face, so close that their beards were almost touching, engaged in a conversation which seemed as passionate as it was low-pitched. It appeared to me that Agamemnon was not the only one under pressure here. The already nervous servant turned and very sensibly vanished, leaving me in the modest courtyard, unobserved by the two men, alone and hesitant as to what to do.

***

'What do you mean you blame me! It was your idea!' snarled Menelaus.

'Born out of desperation! Once I'd thought it through I saw how impossible it was!' spat Agamemnon.

'That's easy to say now!' his brother sneered.

'None of this has been easy! Not then, not now!' raged the High King.

'You're the same as all the others!' said Menelaus. 'When you're trying to win the votes then nothing will be too much trouble! You're as reliable as the sunrise and you promise to shine on everyone all day! But when you actually get the position you want and find you have to make some hard decisions and sacrifices to hold onto it then it's one excuse after another! I saw your face when you managed to get all these men with their thousand ships here to agree that you should be in over-all command! But it's changed now, hasn't it? Now that we're all stuck with no prospect of getting to Troy and rescuing my Helen! Not now that there's talk of whole armies turning around and heading for home, leaving you to stew in your own juice. Now that reliable sunrise has become as inconsistent as the moon. Which, aptly enough, has been waning for the last seven nights!'

'You're a fine one to talk! Look around you!' hissed Agamemnon. 'Take a good look at all these men assembled here ready to fight and die! And for what? Because you couldn't hold on to your *Helen*!' The way he said her name was a sneer. 'And now that she's left you for someone younger, better-looking and more entertaining in bed, you suddenly want her back! It's pathetic. And look what I have to weigh in the balance!'

'Don't flatter yourself!' growled Menelaus. 'Most of the Kings have brought their armies here because Odysseus had the brilliant idea of making everyone who wanted to marry Helen swear to protect her and the man she finally chose. She chose me and they're here for me! Just because they allowed you to worm your way into the High King's chair doesn't mean you're in charge. You have to earn that right and keep doing so, day in and day out! It's called leadership! And all this time-wasting, prevaricating and double-dealing just isn't enough! You've got to grasp the nettle or give up all your pretentions to overall command! And just because you've got Clytemnestra here to hide behind isn't going to make you look any stronger! Any more decisive!'

'You know I sent a message to her telling her to stay in Mycenae until she heard further…' Some of the fire had gone out of Agamemnon now.

'But the message didn't get through, did it?' Menelaus sensed victory.

'No! It didn't! And I wonder how that happened!' Agamemnon demanded suspiciously.

'You know how it happened! You *saw* how it happened!' Spat Menelaus.

'I don't mean how a dead man didn't deliver it. I know a dead man couldn't deliver it. I just want to know who it was that stopped the dead man from delivering it; stopped him living into the bargain!'

'*Hello*,' said a new voice from immediately behind me. 'Who are you?'

I turned, and there, less than an arm's length away from me, was the most beautiful young woman I had ever seen.

Her eyes were huge and hazel, her hair a tumble of gilded copper, her nose was as straight as an arrow and the delicate barb of her nostrils pointed down to a full, red-lipped mouth which at the moment was smiling quizzically, showing a dimple at each corner that matched the cleft in her determined chin.

'Rhapsode…' I managed. Which though was pretty accomplished considering I could neither breathe nor swallow.

'Oh!' said the young woman. 'Are you to sing for us tonight? May I hear some of the song you have prepared?'

'I must ask the High King first,' I managed, the words feeling like a lumpy foreign language in my mouth.

'Well, let's ask him now! Father!' She called.

Agamemnon turned. All the anger and frustration which has been so clear in his tone and on his face, melting away at once.

'Yes my darling Iphigenia,' he said. 'What is it?'

iii

*'Aphrodite, subtle of soul and deathless daughter of Zeus, weaver of wiles, I pray thee do not slay my dreams, neither with care, dread Mistress, nor with anguish. But in pity hasten, come now from afar when my voice implores thee. Leave your father's Olympian house. Come flying to my aid.' Thus sang the love-stuck Orpheus as he plucked the strings of his lyre and sang to lovely Eurydice, daughter of Apollo, in the golden days when first he became enchanted and she went dancing through the hills and fields her feet lent wings by his words…'* I sang, keeping my eyes closed, not as an aid to concentration but because if I opened them I would be unable to look away from the princess – and I was certain that her father would not be too pleased at having lowly rhapsodes staring at his favourite daughter.

'That's enough,' he said as I reached the end of the opening stanza. 'I'm not at all sure that a song about a poet who according to the legend has to venture into the kingdom of Hades in a futile attempt to retrieve lost love is at all suitable! Especially not given what happened to Orpheus in the end!'

'Oh father!' said the princess chidingly. 'You weren't listening! It is about how young Orpheus first falls in love with Euridice when she was little more than a girl – hardly any older than me! The song describes how she dances through the fields as he plays and sings his love for her and even the trees bend down to hear; long before she trod on one of Artemis' vipers and all the sadness began! It is one of the greatest loves of all! It's so beautiful it made me cry! Oh please let him sing it! Such a lovely song and such a clever idea: a poet singing a song about a poet singing a song...'

'Oh! Very well! But if your mother thinks as I do it will be up to you to explain its suitability to her and I warn you, young lady, you won't find her so easy to persuade. Now off you go. And rhapsode, you may report to Oikonomos after you have bathed, changed into a clean tunic and found a himation better suited to the occasion!'

The princess vanished into the women's quarters and I bagged my harp then ran down the hill to *Thalassa* where, by the grace of the gods, I did indeed have a clean tunic and a formal himation, both of which I had worn at the feast where Artemis' sacred stag had been eaten. At the High King's special and specific order, apparently. Another tit-bit of information I stored away at the back of my mind to discuss with Odysseus when the time was right.

I had bathed in the blessedly cool sea, changed into the clothing suggested by the High King and was making my way back up the hill from *Thalassa* when, not quite by accident, I fell in with Odysseus who was also on his way to the feast with the massive oarsman Elpenor in attendance. The evening was hot and humid, the sky high and sultry despite the stars scattered across it and the promise of a rising moon, little more than a fingernail of waning light now. 'So, Captain,' I said, 'do you know who the princess has come here to marry?'

'I do. But before you ask your next question, I must warn you that I have sworn not to reveal his identity. The queen and the princess wish to go about matters in their own way and the queen particularly wishes to speak to the prospective bridegroom before anything else is announced.'

'That's good,' I said without thinking.

Odysseus chuckled. 'Worried that the announcement would overshadow your performance, eh? You rhapsodes are all the same!'

'Did you hear about what happened to Agamemnon's rhapsode Sophos?' I asked.

'I heard something…'

But before the conversation could go any further Prince Palamedes joined us and I naturally fell back to walk beside Elpenor as befitted my station. Palamedes as usual didn't really register my presence – or, I assumed, that of Elpenor. Whether the massive oarsman was tactful enough to close his ears to the conversation of his betters, I had no idea. I certainly did not, because the conversation was far too interesting.

*** 

'So,' said Palamedes, 'are you expecting to take over the High King's investigation into the death of the sacred stag and the girl from the Temple of Artemis once more?'

'If the High King asks me to.'

'And the death of Sophos? Agamemnon is far more upset about that of course, especially given the circumstances.'

'I really haven't had time to consider the case.'

'Of course you haven't. Agamemnon hasn't asked me to get involved yet either – though it will naturally climb higher on the list of his concerns when the current festivities are over and that pretty little princess of his is brided and bedded in due form by which ever royal stallion has been selected for her.'

*Not you then*, I thought; though I realised at once that

Palamedes was devious enough to be playing a double game here.

'Especially,' observed Odysseus as I entertained these thoughts, 'if the man who killed the stag has not been unmasked by then and the wind has not begun to blow. Perhaps the High King is planning that the drama circulating around these mysterious murders will distract the armies for a few more days. Hold them here, no matter how impatient they become, in the hope that this dead calm will pass.'

'Hmmm,' said Palamedes. 'So the wedding is to distract us, especially I assume, because everyone is bursting to know the bridegroom's secret identity. And as soon as that distraction ends at the temple and the bridal bed, the murders will immediately present another distraction…'

'Compounded, once again, by the secret identity of the man at the heart of it. A secret murderer in parallel to the anonymous bridegroom. Then what, I wonder, if the wind still refuses to co-operate.'

'More murders, perhaps,' suggested Palamedes.

Palamedes said it seemingly without having thought, certainly without having considered the implications. But the casual suggestion started a new train of thought in my mind that was truly unsettling. What if Agamemnon himself was responsible for the murders – as the two kings had suggested while bandying their ideas about - to distract the restless and impatient army from their increasingly dangerous desire to go home? And, should that truly shocking notion have any basis in reality, then who would be next to die?

It was at this point in my reasoning that I remembered how high I had stood on the list of men the Rat wanted to kill. The Rat, whose corpse had been carried not to King Aias or Palamedes for disposal, but to Menelaus – whose tent stood so close to his brother's that not even Ikaros would have been able to say which brother the dead murderer was destined for. Not with any certainty. So, suddenly and unexpectedly, it seemed that I was once again in deadly danger. Or, more accurately, perhaps, I thought, I could now see and understand the danger I had always been standing in. Almost unconsciously, I quickened my pace, catching up with my captain and protector. Just as I did so, however, Diomedes fell in at Odysseus' right shoulder and Aias fell in at Palamedes' left. Attendants came beside Elpenor and myself, so that as we arrived at Agamemnon's tent, there was quite a crowd of us.

All the others paused in the reception area immediately outside the megaron, but I went straight on through, more confident of my place and looking for Oikonomos. The chief steward was, inevitably, fussing around the fire pit. His underlings had prepared the seating, again at his direction. He had to be aware of the seating plan because it was part of his duties to conduct the guests to their allotted places. He was also in charge of cooking the meat and fish. Agamemnon habitually demanded perfection and the presence of Clytemnestra would no doubt make those demands even more forceful; a thoroughly complicated situation because when the guests actually arrived in the megaron ready to eat, lay entirely at the whim of the High King and his Queen and therefore far beyond the chief steward's control.

But, I reasoned, things might not be as desperate for Oikonomos as they seemed at first glance. Just as the chief steward wanted to be sure that the food he served was at the peak of perfection, so the High King and his Queen as hosts of the feast, wanted their guests to enjoy their food at the peak of perfection also. So a certain amount of secret scurrying seemed to occur as the chief steward's acolytes and Agamemnon's attendants passed messages between the two men designed to warn one of any possible delays and the other of the readiness of the feast.

Everything was proceeding as planned, therefore, until disaster struck. The messenger briefed by the chief steward took off like a hare from his master's side, heading past the fire pit for the doorway into the reception area while all his colleagues worked with the practised ease of Myrmidons – each man having a task and doing it perfectly. But the messenger slipped. I did not see how it happened but one moment he was hurrying towards the doorway, the next he was rolling around on the expensive flooring trying to beat out the flames consuming his arm and shoulder. Oikonomos took control at once, pouring water on the screaming servant but it was clear that his messenger was no longer in any fit state to approach the High King. The steward's gaze raked round the megaron. It was obvious that he could spare no-one. Until his eye fell on me. 'Rhapsode!' he snapped. 'Go and inform the High King and Queen Clytemnestra that the feast is ready!'

iv

I had talked with Agamemnon that afternoon with a very uncertain outcome and I was hesitating in the outer area, summoning up the courage to do so once again, when Princess Iphigenia spotted me. 'Rhapsode!' she said, approaching with a smile. 'Shouldn't you be in the megaron either at you seat for the feast or on your stool for the song, but in any case taking this opportunity for a final rehearsal?'

'I should, Princess,' I croaked. 'But Oikonomos sent me through to inform your parents that the food is ready.'

'And you came! You are an unusual rhapsode! Sophos would never have dreamed of demeaning himself in such a manner!'

'Have I done wrong, Princess?' I asked, aghast.

Her chuckle in answer was deep and throaty. 'I hesitate to speak ill of the dead, but if Sophos had been commanded to carry your message from Oikonomos to my parents, the feast would have been ashes long before we were informed that it was ready!'

'Oh...' I looked around. The High King was deep in conversation with Leonteus of Argissa and Queen Clytemnestra was talking to Menelaus. She was turned towards me and the face I could see over the King of Sparta's shoulder was the second most lovely in the place; the third loveliest below Olympus, perhaps, after those of her daughter and her sister. 'Come,' said Iphigenia imperiously and set off towards her father her gilded ringlets bouncing. By the grace of the gods, Leonteus backed away just before the Princess and I arrived. He was replaced by Odysseus and Diomedes. This fact gave me further courage; of course, the princess's presence would be recognised no matter who was talking with her father. But now my presence would be registered as well. I need not have worried, of course. 'Excuse me, majesties,' said Iphigenia courteously but irresistibly. 'Oikonomos has requested that King Odysseus' rhapsode inform the High King my father that the feast is ready when he and my mother the Queen would care to lead the guests through.'

Once again I felt the weight of the High King's gaze resting on me. 'Is this so?' he demanded, as though questioning the truthfulness of the Princess' pronouncements was a commonplace matter.

'It is, Spudeos Basileus,' I said quietly. 'The messenger Oikonomos first sent to inform you fell into the fire and so I came in his place.'

'Are we to eat roasted slave at this feast as well?' demanded a voice that contrived to be both soft and icy. 'It certainly smells as though we are!'

'Oh Mother!' sighed Iphigenia. 'The poor man must have been hurt quite badly. We should be thanking the rhapsode here for stepping into the breach so swiftly and willingly.'

Those fathomless brown eyes rested on me for a moment. 'You seem to have made a friend of my daughter, rhapsode,' she said. 'She has been singing the praises of your wedding-song all afternoon. I suggest you enjoy the honour as speedily as you can, however - you will lose her to another so swiftly.'

Agamemnon grunted at the words. 'Are you ready, my dear?' he asked.

'Of course, My Lord,' she answered. 'King Diomedes, would you please escort the Princess Iphigenia to the table?'

'Of course, Majesty. I would be honoured.'

I stepped back as Diomedes stepped forward. *It's not you either*, I thought, not least because, as he had already mentioned, Diomedes was recently married. Then I waited while all the royal guests went through, were greeted by Oikonomos and his assistants and guided to their allotted places. I was content to bring up the rear because, although I had not rehearsed my song as the princess suggested, I had already been in the megaron and I knew my place.

***

The evening passed pleasantly enough. The mysterious section of kid I was served turned out to be well-cooked and surprisingly tasty; a considerable step up from the shattered shank. My song passed uninterrupted even though King Nestor and several other Argonauts of that elder generation had actually known Orpheus. Neither of Iphigenia's parents questioned the suitability of my song, and although there was no jewelled dagger this time, the smile that the Princess flashed in my direction was worth more to me than Achilles' golden armour, let alone a gaudy dagger. Precious also was Odysseus' 'Well done lad!' and Diomedes' hand on my shoulder as we finally left Agamemnon's tent and began to make our way towards the kings' accommodation and *Thalassa*. As the murmur of conversation fell away behind us, the night sounds closed down in its place. Gulls called sleepily. Cicadas chirruped despite the rapidly cooling air. Owls swooped and called, ghostly in the pallid starlight.

King Nestor joined us just as one of the owls swooped inquisitively above our heads. The ancient king gestured to the pale outline of a bird hanging silently low above us. 'That's Athena keeping a close eye on us,' he said.

'It's Artemis I'm worried about, Majesty,' I replied. The moment I spoke, a low grunting noise came from beyond the rubbish heaps up the hill on our right. 'That'll be Artemis now,' said Odysseus. He slapped his scarred thigh, 'Let's hope it's a smaller relation to the boar that gave me this, eh?'

'Ha!' scoffed the old man. 'If you're talking about Artemis and boars, you should have seen the Calydonian Boar she sent to revenge herself on King Oeneus of Calydon when he failed to do her sufficient honour at a sacrifice! Monstrous it was, all black bristles and red, burning eyes, and as for its tusks! You ask Machaon or Podialirius if you don't believe me, their father King Asclepius was there with the rest of us and that pretty little creature Atalanta who drew first blood even though she was a woman!'

'Or,' Odysseus reminded him gently, 'You could ask me. My father King Laertes was also there and he told me all about it at great length on many occasions!'

'It came at you like an army ready for battle,' Nestor continued undaunted. 'Hairs bristling like spears, breast just one impenetrable black shield, eyes like hot coals, mouth spitting fire and burning drool. Tusks as sharp as swords and the length of an elephant's…'

Nestor was still talking when our little group broke up. He and Diomedes led their servants towards their tents and at last only Odysseus, Elpenor and I were left, strolling pensively onwards towards Odysseus' tent. 'It's late,' said the king as we approached. 'And the moon isn't giving any light tonight. Why don't you bed down here. There's plenty of room. I'll come aboard *Thalassa* with you in the morning and you can show me what you discovered while I was in Ithaka. There's space for you too, Elpenor. The more of us bedded down there, the safer I'll feel – just in case that boar we heard earlier really is as big as the monster Artemis sent to Calydon!'

He was joking of course, but in the way that such things sometimes happen, Artemis must have been listening to him, or, if not the Goddess herself than that dangerous trickster Hermes. We had bedded down and, speaking for myself at least, fallen instantly into a deep sleep. It seemed to me therefore that I no sooner closed my eyes than Odysseus was shaking my shoulder, his frowning face gilded by the light of a lamp-flame. 'Something's happened,' he said. 'They're asking for me to come at once. I thought I'd bring you along as usual.'

I sat up immediately. Elpenor was already shrugging on his tunic and I reached for mine at once. It didn't occur to me to ask what the matter was or who had called for Odysseus until we were walking purposefully up the hill with the rose-fingered promise of dawn lightening the sky above the ship-crowded bay behind us. We were being guided by the man who had summoned Odysseus and I recognised him as the frog-faced servant Oikonomos had sent to invite Achilles to the feast. I frowned, trying to work out what message the servant could have brought that could summon Odysseus from his bed like this. And then with a chill of revelation I began to suspect. But the truth is that I did not suspect the half of what we were just about to find.

The body was lying face down in the clear area between the topmost tents and the rubbish piles. The head and shoulders were on the downslope, the soles of the footwear pointing up at the Groves of Artemis above. The first thing I noticed were the hands. Their fingers were clawed into the dry brown grass as though whoever this was had been trying to pull itself along when he died. And, sure enough, there was a short trail of blood blackening the ground between the dead knees, stretching back from beneath the body almost as far as the ankles. It seemed clear that the dead man had not been touched. To a certain extent there was little need to interfere with him because the head was turned sideways to present a familiar profile. Even though the face was made strange at first glance by the contortion of the dead features, it was easy enough to recognise.

'Oikonomos,' I said. 'Agamemnon's not going to like this. First his rhapsode and then his chief steward.

'But what in the name of the gods has happened to him?'

wondered Elpenor.

'We'll need to turn him over to be certain, but I have a pretty good idea,' said Odysseus grimly.

Elpenor, the frog-faced servant and I took hold of the corpse and rolled him over. So the first pink light of dawn revealed the great slashes that opened his thighs from knee to groin down as deep as the bone. And the sideways rent that had torn his belly so that his guts were on the point of cascading out to join the great wave of blood he left smeared across the grass. 'What did this?' wondered Elpenor, shaken.

Perhaps it was a coincidence, but when he stooped to lower his lamp for a closer look, Odysseus put his left hand on the scar running up his own thigh as he answered his oarsman's question. 'It was a boar,' he said.


v

Agamemnon sat in the High King's seat he had occupied at last night's feast but the table that had fronted him was gone. He was wrapped in a cloak, having been called from his bed but he still contrived to look regal. Regal and in some state which existed beyond outrage and naked fury; a state surely bordering madness for which no word had yet been invented. Odysseus and I stood before him. Elpenor was standing guard over the body, making sure it remained undisturbed until we returned for a closer examination. Palamedes had been summoned. There were messengers also speeding towards Aulis and the Temple of Artemis. Nestor appeared, though I didn't realise he had been invited. So did Diomedes, who came to stand beside Odysseus. Queen Clytemnestra arrived, with a couple of personal servants still fussing over the ebony perfection of her hair. But to be fair, she could have exchanged her hairstyle with Medusa the Gorgon and she would still have been heart-stoppingly lovely. She was also icily remote, like the peak of the highest northern mountain in midwinter. Hardly surprising under the circumstances, I thought. Her gaze swept across us and I realised what had put

Medusa into my mind. It was a wonder we did not all turn to stone.

'First Sophos,' grated the High King, 'and now Oikonomos! What is going on here?'

'First,' said Odysseus quietly, 'the sacred deer and the young priestess. Then Sophos. And now Oikonomos. We might also observe the deaths of nameless man in the grip of a bear and his companion called the Rat poisoned by a viper.'

'And are you tying all these various deaths together?' enquired Clytemnestra.

'I have no idea if they should be tied together, Majesty, but I suggest we should not be too quick to separate them.'

'Well,' snapped Agamemnon, 'now you're back – without your Cephallenian fleet I notice – you can look into the more recent outrages. Those which involved my servants. Bears and rats need hardly concern us. Ah, here is Palamedes. He can continue his enquiry into who might have killed the so-called sacred stag and that stupid girl who seems to have thrown herself in front of it just at the worst possible moment!'

'It may be that Palamedes and I will have to work together,' warned Odysseus. And the tone of his voice made it clear that this was a genuine warning. Palamedes was brilliant but arrogant. The bad blood that had lain between him and Odysseus ever since Palamedes had revealed Odysseus' attempt to feign madness by throwing the infant Telemachus onto the ground immediately in front of his father's plough-blade would never be settled until one or the other of them was dead. It was only through the grace of the gods that the little prince had survived the brutal test of his father's sanity. And, personal animus aside, I could see Odysseus' point – Agamemnon still did not want the man guilty of that first outrage unmasked because there was little doubt that the truth would destroy the increasingly strained accord that was holding the entire army together. On the other hand, he most certainly wanted the men who had killed Sophos and the animal that had all-but gutted Oikonomos caught and given the most agonisingly appropriate punishment possible.

It was at this point that the delegation from Aulis arrived. As chance would have it, Father led the envoys. His gaze swept over me with a smile the faintest ghost of a wink. 'Well, Basileus,' he said to Agamemnon, never one to give more respect than he felt he owed and markedly parsimonious in the matter of royal titles. 'What can the good people of Aulis do for you on this occasion? More lambs and kids? A ram perhaps or a good big billygoat?'

'I have called you here,' snarled the High King, 'about a boar!'

'Ah. Boars could be a problem, Majesty. They are like bears and certain stags: sacred to Artemis, and…'

'I don't want to cook one!' roared the High King. 'I want to know whether your town has ever been troubled by bears and boars coming down out of the forest…'

'Out of the Groves of the Goddess,' said Father, utterly unmoved by Agamemnon's anger. 'No, I can't say that we have, Majesty. But then we in Aulis live under the protection of the Goddess and remain in consequence, safe from her creatures. On the other hand I have to observe that there has never been so much temptation piled all over the upper slopes to entice them out. I know a bear is said to have attacked one of your soldiers a few days ago. Are you telling me that a boar has done some damage now?'

'It has killed my Chief Steward Oikonomos! Gutted him like a fish!'

Father took a dramatic step back, his hands flung up in horror. 'I am shocked, Majesty! Aghast! We have never had anything like that happen; certainly not in my memory! I didn't even know there were any wild boars left up there these days. Have you discussed the matter with the High Priestess?'

'No!' came a voice that was just as icy as Queen Clytemnestra's. 'But believe you me, he's just about to!'

High Priestess Karpathia swept into the tent, with Ikaros immediately behind her.

\*\*\*

'Well?' snapped Agamemnon, turning his fury upon Karpathia, 'are there wild boars up there?'

'Not to my knowledge,' the High Priestess snapped back. 'Ikaros? You know the Groves of the Goddess better than anyone. Have you seen any wild boars up there?'

'I have seen pigs and piglets and assume there must be boars as well. But I cannot be certain, Basilissa,' answered the old huntsman. 'I had assumed that there were no bears left up there either but I was obviously mistaken in that belief.'

I opened my mouth to join the discussion but Diomedes spoke over me as Odysseus was frowning pensively apparently lost in thought. 'We heard a pig rooting through the piles of waste as we walked back to our tents after the feast,' he said. 'I couldn't swear whether the animal was a sow or a boar, but I'm certain it was there.'

'Bears, boars, vipers, sacred stags... What sort of a menagerie do you keep up in those woods?' wondered Clytemnestra. The fact that the question was asked quietly did not rob it of its chilling edge.

Karpathia's attention moved from the High King to the Queen. It was as though the Myrmidons, having considered one weak spot in the Trojan walls, had now turned their hostile attention to another. 'We keep everything that is sacred to the Goddess,' she answered, equally quietly. 'Artemis choses to manifest herself in many forms and put her blessings on others. All of them are sacred.'

'I think the Goddess should be made aware,' Palamedes very clearly spoke for Agamemnon who was apparently too angry to speak for himself, 'that if she or any of her pets choose to manifest themselves outside her sacred groves, then they only have themselves to blame if we kill them either for protection, sport or food!'

I had never seen an expression quite like the smile with which Karpathia reacted to this. It was not even remotely attractive or humorous. In the depths behind it lurked an outrage that matched even Agamemnon's. 'The Oracle and I will put your argument to the Goddess as soon as I return to the temple,' she said. 'You will hear from one of us in due course.'

'And you'd better hope,' said Ikaros who challenged even Father in his unwillingness to bow before royalty, 'that when you do hear, it's from the Oracle or the High Priestess. You really don't want to hear directly from the Goddess herself any more than you already have!' The silence that followed this pronouncement was just long enough to establish the stillness of the windless morning outside.

'I've had more than enough of the Goddess' threats!' snapped Agamemnon. 'Let's get on here! First and most importantly I want to know all about how Sophos and Oikonomos met their ends! King Odysseus, would you kindly give these matters your closest attention at once.'

Odysseus and Diomedes left Agamemnon's accommodation side by side. I followed them. Nestor stayed with Palamedes to advise the High King. As we came out into the bright, still morning, Kalkhas the Soothsayer and Aias both hurried past, ready to join the increasingly acrimonious discussion in the tent. 'So,' said Odysseus, 'I'd be grateful if you would tell me the details you have discovered about Sophos' murder in a while. In the meantime, logic dictates that we should begin with the dead man who has been most recently killed. Being gored to death by a boar appears at first sight simply to be a random accident. It is only the involvement of the Goddess that seems to make this all part of a pattern. And of course the problem is that I do not actually believe that the Goddess is really involved at all.'

'Still, if she is,' said Diomedes, 'there might still be a pattern to discover.'

'I'm not certain I see the logic in that approach,' said Odysseus. 'Even if we do find an apparent pattern in these events, it's still no proof that the Goddess...'

As Odysseus said this, we passed Oikonomos' tent. I knew it was the right tent because my frog-faced friend was hopping from foot to foot outside it. 'Perhaps this would be an opportune moment to have an initial look in Oikonomos' accommodation,' I suggested. 'The body won't be going anywhere. Not with Elpenor guarding it.'

'Very well,' said Odysseus. 'It is an efficient use of our time if nothing else. And the less time I waste on this, the more chance I will have to discover how it all started, whether Agamemnon and Palamedes want me to or not.'

As Odysseus said this, he stooped to enter the cramped accommodation of the High King's Chief Steward. Diomedes followed and I followed him. There wasn't really room for the three of us but at least it was clear immediately that Oikonomos occupied the tent alone. I suspected that his underlings bunked in two, three or even four to a tent. There was a makeshift bed, much like the beds Machaon had in the hospital. Travelling panniers no doubt full of clothes and other necessaries, something amongst which seemed to be giving off a strongly unpleasant smell. A makeshift table with clay tablets on it. The tablets were covered in the sort of marks I had tried to learn while working in one of my father's storehouses with a record keeper from Pylos. The marks were used to keep basic accounts of supplies whose details were impossible to remember accurately. He said they were called 'writing'.

But the thing of most interest lay in the corner of the tent just beyond the bed-foot. It looked at first glance as though Oikonomos had chosen to cover a small bush with a couple of his cloaks and I immediately wondered whether this was some way of drying the garments out. But then I remembered that there had been no rain since the storms were replaced by this sweltering calm.

These thoughts were fleeting at best, however, for Odysseus reached over and pulled the coverings loose. To reveal the gilded antlers that had once adorned the head of Artemis' sacred stag.

## 7 - The Princess and the Priestess

i

Oikonomos lay face-up on Machaon's table. He was naked, lacking even the usual covering to protect his modesty. His eyes stared sightlessly at the tent-roof, wide with shock and horror. Some philosophers believed that the last thing he had seen was drawn forever there. But we had no need of that final vision, I thought: we knew exactly what the last thing he had seen was. The expression frozen on his face told us all we needed to know about its size and fearsomeness. His mouth gaped as though he was screaming but of course no sound was coming out of it. The fact there had been nothing coming out of it on an earlier occasion was starting to exercise our minds as we discussed how the poor man met his brutal end.

The flesh of both thighs sagged open from groin to knee, revealing the white sticks of his thigh bones, though the pale columns were smeared with dark blood. The gaping flesh was clotted with it – a mixture of blood and dust from the brick-dry ground. There was a larger smear of the stuff on his right side than there was on his left, which had been repeated more thickly on the tunic Machaon had just finished removing. At least his current position allowed the snakes' nest of his intestines to remain inside him, contained in the cup formed by the bones of his hips and pubis, even though the muscular wall that normally stood in front of them had been ripped as wide as his thighs. The flesh had been folded down over his genitals like the skirts of a tunic.

'It must have been a fearsome beast to have done this,' said Machaon. 'Almost as large as the boar Artemis sent to Calydon. And yet there were no tracks you say?'

'None,' answered Odysseus. He turned to Ikaros who had been summoned from the High Priestess' side to add his expertise as a hunter and tracker. But, on Odysseus' specific order, we had not mentioned the gilded antlers in the dead Chief Stewards' tent to him, suspecting that the High Priestess might demand their return before we had finished examining them.

'The ground's too hard,' said Ikaros now. 'This weather has set it solid. It's like rock.'

'And nobody heard anything,' the physician persisted.

'We heard a pig rooting around in the rubbish mounds,' I confirmed, glancing across at Diomedes. 'But I don't think anyone else heard anything. Or saw anything.'

Machaon shook his head. 'If something was doing this to me, I'd be yelling my head off...'

Without a word, Odysseus gestured to Ikaros and me so the pair of us lifted the dead shoulders. The head rolled back like a surprisingly weighty ball. 'If you feel the back of his skull,' said the Captain, reaching over and cupping the thick-haired curve in his hand to show what he meant. Then he nodded to Machaon, stepping back so the other man could feel what he was talking about. When the physician did so he said, 'That's quite a bump. You think he was unconscious? Lying down?'

'I'd gone down after putting my spear in my boar's shoulder. Then it did this to me.' Odysseus moved his leg so that the long scar running up his thigh came into view. 'You don't have to be standing up to get gored.'

'So,' said Machaon pensively. 'It surprised him.'

'Charged him down,' added Diomedes grimly. 'Winded him and knocked him unconscious when the back of his head hit the rock-hard ground. Then it went to work.'

It must have been guided by the Goddess, I thought, in revenge for taking the antlers. The boar that had gored Odysseus had been fighting its hunters. But why a boar should just attack a passing stranger without divine prompting was something that exercised my mind. I remained silent, though, as the conversation continued around me.

'But you found him face down,' said Machaon. 'He must have come to and turned over.'

'The thicker blood on his right side certainly suggests it,' said Odysseus and Ikaros nodded his agreement.

'He could only have done that, I assume, after the boar had gone back to the Groves of the Goddess because there are no wounds on his back. Why not call for help then?'

'Maybe it was just too late,' said Ikaros. 'Maybe he couldn't get enough breath. Only the gods know what having your belly torn open like that would do to your ability to breathe, let alone shout. And if the length of the bloodstain is anything to go by, he had almost no time at all. One convulsive heave moved him the length of his legs downhill and that was that.'

'You're right,' said Odysseus. 'That must be what happened. One death explained at least. But I'm not going to report back to Agamemnon until I've had a chance to think this whole thing through.' He looked around at us all. 'We'll just have to hope that Agamemnon is so caught up in the wedding preparations that he doesn't bother to keep too close an eye on us and what we're doing.'

'Because,' said Diomedes, 'there's something going on here that we still haven't fathomed. Something apart from everything the High King doesn't want us looking too closely into. Something Palamedes and that murderous little scum Aias with his extra private army of murderers have been told to keep us well away from.'

'I agree,' said Odysseus. 'But I'm not quite certain yet who's giving Aias his orders.'

'Well,' said Diomedes bracingly. 'There's only one way to find that out as far as I can see.'

'Yes,' said Odysseus, straightening and purposely misunderstanding his friend's warlike suggestion. 'We have to go right back to basics and think the whole thing through once more.'

*\*\**

'So, said Odysseus a little later as full day gathered around *Thalassa* and Elpenor brought a simple breakfast to us as we talked, allowing the food to share table space with the contents of my bag-full of clues. 'Let's look at it right from the beginning – as far as we understand the sequence of events.' Having said that, he fell silent, pushing the skull one way, the foreleg another; holding up the two very different arrow-heads and the two equally different knives.

In the absence of anything immediate from the Captain or Diomedes, I leaped into the breach. The ship's forecastle had been chosen for our secret deliberations because – unlike Agamemnon's tent for example - it was almost impossible to spy on. Not even the sharpest ear could hear anything through that sold hull, especially with the rumble of the lazy foam running to and fro along its seaward sides. 'So,' I said. 'Agamemnon and Menelaus arrive here with their armies and are joined by all the greatest kings in Achaea.'

'Or their most trusted offspring,' added Diomedes. 'That's the most powerful gathering of royalty since the suitors for Helen's hand all got together at Sparta the best part of ten years ago. I was there myself, though I was hardly more than a boy.'

'One of them, we don't know which,' I persisted, 'seems to have asked for Princess Iphigeneia's hand in marriage. He did so in secret and for some reason that secret has been kept by the widening circle of people who know the truth.' I looked pointedly at Odysseus, but he appeared to be so deep in thought that he didn't hear me.

'The weather was bad,' mused Diomedes, warming to this game of fitting what facts we knew into a story we thought convincing. 'The army was not yet fully formed or ready. Agamemnon thought that a royal wedding would pass the time in a positive manner. As soon as the proposal of marriage was made, he sent a message to summon Clytemnestra and Iphigenia.'

'In the mean-time,' I chimed in once more, 'someone killed

both the sacred deer and the young priestess Nephele. Suddenly Artemis was demanding the sacrifice of a child in recompense or she would hold the entire Achaean force here indefinitely. The weather closed down immediately in such a manner that all sorts of people from royalty to soldiery began to give some credence to the messages passed on from the Oracle by the High Priestess.'

I paused for breath and looked at my pensive audience before I continued. 'That changed everything. Given those new circumstances, the camp was the last place under Olympus that Agamemnon wanted any child of his to be. So he made plans to send a second message, via Sophos his rhapsode, while the High Priestess asked you, Captain, to find the man who killed the deer and started the curse. The second message he sent to Queen Clytemnestra was inevitably quite long and complicated. There was a lot of explaining to be done in it – which is why he got his rhapsode to learn it off by heart as though it was one of the poet's songs. When he was satisfied that the rhapsode had the message off exactly as he wanted, he sent him hurrying to Mycenae, believing he had acted in good time to stop his wife and daughter from arriving.'

'Then Agamemnon realised…' began Diomedes, picking up the thread of the narrative.

'… prompted by Menelaus, I believe,' I added.

'…that if the man who was unmasked as having killed the stag, and who therefore must sacrifice one of his children, was one of the more powerful kings, it was entirely likely that the guilty king, whoever it was, would at the least take his army home and might even start a civil war here before he gave in to Artemis' demands. Especially if Agamemnon tried to enforce the Goddess' ruling. A complete disaster either way.'

'So the High King sent you home, Captain,' I continued, 'and used that as an excuse to give the enquiry over to Palamedes who would guarantee the outcome that

Agamemnon wanted and keep the High Priestess happy for the moment at least, while the High King in the meantime agreed to get rid of the evidence by holding a feast and eating it.'

'But,' said Diomedes to Odysseus, 'your absence also cleared the ground for the Rat and his friends to make sure that our young rhapsode here had not learned too much while he was assisting you. And it had also already given someone the opportunity to stop Agamemnon's second message getting to Clytemnestra by shooting poor old Sophos the messenger and cutting his throat for good measure.'

'That must have happened some time before the feast,' I reasoned. 'Because that was the feast at which I sang my first song and was given the deer's broken leg to eat. Which prompted me to look further into the matter…'

'… and put him at the top of the Rat's murder list,' concluded Diomedes. 'Someone, probably *not* the High King but probably whoever was in ultimate charge of the Rat, sent him an easily-identifiable dagger as a gift for singing such a good song. The dagger allowed the Rat and his friends to identify him all too easily. I had no idea that being a rhapsode was such a dangerous calling. Please don't ask me to look after any more rhapsodes, Odysseus. Never. Not ever.'

Odysseus stirred. He gave a brief smile. 'It seems the lad was under the protection of the Goddess in any case,' he observed. 'The first would-be murderer crushed by a bear sacred to Artemis, the Rat finally killed by a viper sacred to Artemis. If Oikonomos had presented the boy with any kind of a threat, the boar would have made it three animals watching out for him, all of them sacred to Artemis.'

ii

'I don't know if Ikaros counts as one of the Goddess' creatures,' I added, 'but it was his slingshot that saved me when the Rat was just about to kill me with the dagger that cut poor Sophos' throat – and nearly took his head into the bargain.'

'It is certain that Sophos was the man carrying the second message to Queen Clytemnestra and that message contradicted the first, commanding her to stay in Mycenae and keep the Princess safe,' said Diomedes. 'Surely we can judge this from Agamemnon's surprise when she appeared. Everything he has done since her arrival has been unplanned reaction to one crisis after another. Which is why, despite his bitter words about your fleet's non-arrival, the High King is actually relieved you have returned, Odysseus. He is still, clearly, chary about unmasking the man who killed the stag but he very much does want to know who killed his rhapsode and his chief steward.'

Odysseus grunted. 'You see what you've done there?' He asked. 'You've linked a death which was obviously a murder with one that is an apparently random animal attack.'

'But surely,' I said, 'If Oikonomos' death is linked to any other deaths it must be linked to the Rat's and his friend who was killed by the bear.'

'By the hand of the Goddess,' said Odysseus. 'As suggested by the fact that he was in possession of her sacred stag's gilded antlers when he died. Yes, you're right.' He stirred himself and demanded abruptly, apparently a propos of nothing, 'I wonder have all the bodies been burned or buried yet.'

'Well, if you're thinking of starting with the first one, you'd better hurry,' said Diomedes. 'And if you're planning to go up to the Temple, this is where our ways part.'

Diomedes had his duties as senior of the three commanders in charge of the four-thousand-man Argive army, and these pulled him away for the rest of the morning while Odysseus and I went to Aulis with Elpenor who put the Ithacan stallions to Odysseus' chariot and drove us up to the Temple. At first the temple precinct seemed deserted. 'Good,' said Odysseus. 'I want to poke around a little.' We left Elpenor holding the horses' heads and walked towards the rear of the temple building. We had never had the opportunity to explore this far before and I was surprised at how abruptly the hillsides stepped up back here. There was a steep slope leading up to a plateau level with the temple's roof where a pyre was being busily erected – which explained the lack of acolytes and priestesses down here. But behind and above this there was another, higher level. On this, an impressive-looking altar was under construction with a familiar figure in charge of the work. 'Is that Kalkhas?' I asked the Captain, squinting to get a clearer view.

'Yes,' he said. 'It is.'

'It is good to see you have returned from Ithaka,' said a familiar voice immediately behind us, 'though of course Ikaros informed me you were back. And you fell in with Queen Clytemnestra on the way. A lucky coincidence...'

'Unless it was once again the hand of the Goddess,' said Odysseus, turning back to face the High Priestess.

'Quite,' said Karpathia. 'You never know. Now, what can the servants of Artemis do for you?'

'I would like to see poor Nephele if such a thing is possible such a long time after her death.'

'It is possible. She is in the cold room beneath the temple, undergoing the final rituals before holy fire transports her anima to the arms of the Goddess herself.' She gestured up towards the funeral pyre. 'A ceremony that is conducted on the first night that the new moon appears in the sky, when just the faintest bow of light can be seen as proof that Artemis the Huntress is at her closest to the earth.'

Odysseus was courteously careful not to point out that Artemis appeared to have a habit of wandering around Aulis and its environs no matter what phase the moon was at. Then Karpathia herself led us off the hill slopes, through the temple and down into an icy vault beneath it, her determined footsteps ringing on the marble floor as we approached the place. There we found the dead priestess lit by a range of lamps, surrounded by increasingly impenetrable shadows.

The golden brightness revealed her to be in a surprising state of preservation – though to be fair all we could see of her was the vague shape of her body beneath a sheet of fine white cloth and her face, which was only visible when an equally fine veil was lifted aside. The poor girl's final expression was one of restful peace. Ointments and potions far beyond my reckoning had been used to bring a faint blush to her cheeks and a lifelike colour to her lips. Her hair was neatly bound in braids secured with ribbons as though she was being prepared for a festival rather than her funeral. Her eyes were closed. I had expected the room to smell of death. It smelt of lavender and rosemary. And of something else – a powerful and quite disgusting smell that was the faintest trace in the background. I knew it but could not identify it. Then Odysseus said quietly, 'Come out into the light, Ikaros. There is no need to be shy - standing guard over the priestess must be a task which honours you as well as her.'

Ikaros stepped forward and the reason for his shyness struck me at once. So far we had only seen him in his hunting attire of dark-furred skin jerkin over substantial tunic with heavy skin-bound boots and thick woollen cloak as conditions required. Now he was dressed as an acolyte to the Goddess in a pure white tunic and golden sandals, his hair oiled into neat curls and encircled with a wreath. Even his beard looked as sleek as the back of an otter. Without a word he resumed the station in which, I assumed, he had been standing, at the foot of the table which bore the corpse.

Odysseus spent some time in silent contemplation of the dead girl, his concentration and silence so deep that he might have been praying to the Goddess himself. Karpathia stood watching him with equal intensity. After a while, however, he stirred and turned to the High Priestess. 'I thank you for your courtesy,' he said quietly. 'And I apologise if we have interrupted any important rituals.'

Then he turned and led the way out to his waiting chariot.

\*\*\*

'It's almost enough to make one believe in the power of the Goddess,' he said as Elpenor guided the horses back towards Aulis.

'What is?' I wondered.

'The way that child has been preserved, so long after her death. Consider – there has been time for the deer that died with her to be skinned, gutted, hung until it was tender and mature, for it to be prepared, cooked and eaten – and all that some days ago. Yet the child who has lain there all that length of time appears merely to have fallen into the lightest slumber. But I hope you observed that on the level above the first level where her pyre is being erected, a sacrificial altar is also being built by Kalkhas; closer still to the sky-dwelling goddess.' He gave a perplexed sigh. Then he continued – as he often did – with a question that seemed to have nothing whatsoever to do with what we had just been discussing. 'Do you think your father will be at home?'

'If he's not at home he'll be at the main warehouse on the docks,' I said. 'Though home is more likely given the weather. His ships can't sail any more than Agamemnon's can.'

'Very well. We will leave Elpenor to take care of the chariot when we reach the agora and then you will guide me to your parents' house.'

We alighted in the agora as the morning ended and Hephaestus high above us guided his golden horses towards the apogee of noon. As soon as the house was in sight I hurried ahead to warn Father and Mother about their royal visitor. Father met Odysseus at the door and welcomed him with quiet courtesy while Mother offered food and drink as xenia, traditional hospitality, demanded. Odysseus accepted gracefully complimenting Mother on the quality of her baking, the tartness of her olives and the sweetness of her figs. Again, this was as tradition demanded but it became clear at once that the captain was after information rather than sustenance. 'When I first met the High Priestess,' he said as soon as the courtesies and the light meal were completed, 'she said she had just come from visiting the unfortunate Nephele's parents. Can you tell me where they live? I would like to ask them a question or two.'

I could have done that without disturbing my parents but I didn't say so. Odysseus rarely did anything without good reason.

Instead, 'Of course,' said Father, guardedly. 'I can take you there myself.'

'That would be most kind.'

Both men stood up.

I stood up as well but Odysseus said, 'I want you to stay here while I do this. I'm sure you have many things you want to talk to your mother about.'

And that was that. Mother and I discussed parental concerns. These were mostly about what it was like working for such a famous king as Odysseus – and might there be room aboard *Thalassa* or in the court at Ithaka for one or more of my brothers. Which I said I doubted thus pleasing Mother not at all. Father returned to find me pacing, confused and impatient. 'Why wouldn't the captain let me come?' I demanded.

Father shot me a dark look. 'Perhaps,' he said, 'your captain thought it improper for a young man to observe his much respected father caught on the horns of a dilemma from which the only possibilities of relief are to break a solemn confidence or tell an outright lie!' He snorted with vexation sounding a little like a startled horse. 'However, he asked me to inform you he wants to discuss matters with you aboard *Thalassa* as soon as you can get there.'

Although there had been no formal repast, my share of the food and drink Mother had offered Odysseus easily replaced my usual midday meal. I hurried out of the house, planning to go through the agora and out of the southern gate therefore. But in the market place itself, I changed my mind. I was bored with all that tramping through the Argive camp.

Instead I headed east, to the dockside packed with slack-sailed merchantmen, many owned by Father, before I turned south and followed the shoreline down onto the beach. I hurried past the familiar fleets, anchored in the bay or beached with their forecastles snugly in the sand while their aft sections sat in the shallows, or also high and dry on the sand if the tide was particularly low. Like *Thalassa*, even the beached ships had pairs of hawsers reaching down from their bows to stakes hammered into the sand, designed to hold the vessels in place even should the weather deteriorate and the tide rise.

So I hurried along the track on which Achilles had outrun the chariot on the morning which now seemed so long in the past. First was the massive Prince Ajax's fleet from Salamis, then the Taphians, the Euphians, the Aeneans' twelve ships – the same number Odysseus was to supply; Nestor's Pylonians came next, then the High King's one hundred Mycenaeans, co-commanded by his brother, Aias' Locrians, the Beoetians, the Athenians led by Theseus' son Acamas, the Argives, *Thalassa* and the other late arrivals – Achilles' Myrmidons – beyond. But as I rushed southward, so I became aware of something else. Something almost intangible; something I was only aware of because I had enjoyed so much of my misspent youth at sea. There was a change in the air. There were the faintest white wisps feathering the solid blue bowl of the early afternoon sky. There was new weather coming. Frowning, I thought back to the conversation the captain and I had held with Karpathia. There was a new moon on the rise and whether or not that meant the Goddess was walking closer to the earth, it often meant the weather was about to change.

Full of this revelation, I hurried towards *Thalassa* and my meeting with Odysseus. Only to be distracted by the sight of Achilles, back from the forced march to Marathon, resplendent in his full gilded armour, his face containing more fury than a thunderstorm, walking purposefully up from the Myrmidon camp. 'Where are you going, majesty?' I asked, hesitantly, taking advantage of the fact that he seemed to like me – and he certainly liked and respected my captain.

He didn't even look at me but he answered. 'To see the High King. It's time we sorted this all out!'

I paused for an instant, torn. Would Odysseus wish me to join him or to follow Achilles? In the end my actions were not dictated by the answer to that question but by my own curiosity.

iii

As I followed Achilles up the hill from *Thalassa* towards Agamemnon's tent, he strode on in angry silence. But after a while he started speaking. At first I thought he was talking to me but eventually I realised he hardly registered my continued presence at all. He was allowing his thoughts to boil over into words, like molten gold in a red-hot crucible. And he was forming those words into the conversation he was planning to have with the High King. 'The forced march to Marathon and back you ordered has proved more than you expected,' he muttered. 'It has established once and for all that the Myrmidons are at their peak. They are as fit and well-prepared as they can possibly be. They know it themselves now. They've started challenging me, asking why we're not finding some way of setting out for Troy. They're burning to go to war and all you can offer them is a wedding!' He lapsed into silence once more. We reached Agamemnon's tent. He stopped, drew himself up, ran his fingers though the golden mane of his hair and then strode forward once again.

The entrance was guarded but as Achilles approached, he ordered, 'Let me pass!' in that ringing, battlefield voice of his. The guards, of course, stepped back at once. He disappeared into the shadows, all gleaming gold, like a shooting star vanishing across the night sky. I, however, was forbidden entry. Apparently idly, but with my ears pricked, I went round to the side of the tent where I had managed to overhear secret conversations in the past. It was still unguarded. I sat, pulled out my lyre and began to tune it, pretending once again to be just an unworldly rhapsode rehearsing.

At once, I heard something I was not expecting. There came the sharp double-clap with which Queen Clytemnestra attracted servants' attention. A moment later a group of them came scurrying out of the front and I assumed any others went out through the megaron into the domestic quarters at the rear. For Clytemnestra clearly wanted a private word with Achilles as their conversation was to prove.

'Prince Achilles,' she said, her tone honeyed. 'I recognised your voice at once.'

'I'm sorry,' answered the young prince stiffly, his mind clearly elsewhere, 'but I'm not sure I know who you are.' A little late in the day, he tried for some charm and gallantry. 'Though I must admit I'm surprised to find someone so lovely in the middle of this huge army.'

'Ah. Of course; there has been no formal introduction. I am Clytemnestra, wife and queen to High King Agamemnon. Mother to his son and daughters.'

'I'm flattered that you want to converse with me, Majesty, but we are alone in private and that is hardly proper. It does not reflect well on your honour nor on mine. Besides, I am here to see your husband on matters to do with the war.'

'So, it's not proper to be talking to the mother of your wife-to-be?' Clytemnestra's tone was at once knowing and teasing. Intimate. Strangely out of place, I thought. 'But we have so much to discuss and agree and so little time in which to prepare your wedding!'

There was a short silence in which I assumed Achilles was as stunned at this news as I was myself. 'But I'm not getting married, Majesty,' he said at last, sounding like a man recently struck by one of Zeus' larger thunderbolts. 'There must be some mistake. I have never proposed to your daughter, never talked to either of the sons of Atreus about any such thing. Besides, although we haven't formalised anything as yet, I have a wife, the Princess Deidamia, King Lycomedes of Skyros' daughter. She's with my mother Queen Thetis in Phthia, awaiting the birth of our child.'

'Indeed there must be some mistake!' Clytemnestra's tone was no longer honeyed. On the contrary, it shook with gathering outrage. 'I find what you are telling me as hard to comprehend as you clearly find what I am telling you! I appear to have been feverishly preparing for a wedding that isn't going to happen!'

'And I have apparently been making proposals I never intended to make. It seems to me, Majesty, that we are both the victims of some sort of plot; though what good anyone could hope to gain from making us both look so foolish I can't begin to guess!'

\*\*\*

I found myself on my feet before I knew it. My hands were sliding my lyre into its bag apparently of their own accord. Then I was off as fast as I could run, heading for that meeting aboard *Thalassa* for which I was already late. The first person I bumped into on the way, however, was Diomedes returning from his general officer duties. 'It's Achilles!' I gasped.

'Achilles?' Diomedes looked around, expecting the Prince of Phthia to appear.

'That Iphigenia is here to marry!' I said as he fell in beside me. 'Except that she isn't!'

'I'm not sure I'm following this,' he said. 'She is and she isn't...'

'Queen Clytemnestra's brought her here because she was told Achilles was proposing marriage. But he wasn't. It was a trick!'

'Who on earth would gain anything from making Clytemnestra and Achilles look foolish?' he wondered.

'No,' I gasped. 'Don't you see? The plan wasn't to make

anyone look foolish. The plan was simply to get Iphigenia here!'

'But why?' demanded Diomedes.

'Because of Artemis' curse,' said Odysseus a few moments later as the three of us sat in the thick-walled forecastle of *Thalassa*. 'The man who killed the stag was advised to bring a child of his own here in case what the Oracle and the High Priestess said was true.'

'But that means the man who shot the priestess and the stag was Agamemnon himself!' I gasped.

'Precisely,' said Odysseus.

'How long have you known?' demanded Diomedes.

'Almost since the beginning. Think about it: Agamemnon was the only one who could have arranged everything in the way it was done. He must have told Menelaus, brother to brother, and Kalkhas the soothsayer, especially when the High Priestess told him why the wind and weather were behaving as they have been. And eventually he told Oikonomos who got rid of the stag – bribed by the golden antlers. But Agamemnon's initial reaction must have been panic. Motivated by shock and horror he acted, probably on the advice of Menelaus and Kalkhas, and certainly before he thought things through. He sent the one message he knew that would get Clytemnestra to bring Iphigenia here – the most flattering proposal of marriage he could imagine. But of course he couldn't tell Achilles because the whole thing was a lie. He came to his senses almost at once and sent the second message. But someone stopped that getting through.'

'Menelaus,' I said. 'If Artemis wasn't satisfied then he could forget about reclaiming his wife.'

'He could wave goodbye to his standing, reputation and honour into the bargain,' added Diomedes.

'I agree,' said Odysseus. 'Menelaus is desperate enough.'

'And he seems to have recruited Aias,' I added, 'who in turn recruited the Rat and his associates. As we learned from the wound in Sophos' throat and the dagger that made it.'

'And when Clytemnestra appeared so unexpectedly,' said Odysseus, 'his first reaction was to send Achilles and the Myrmidons on their forced march to Marathon – hoping no doubt that he'd be able to come up with a solution before Achilles returned. Logical but ineffective, in the final analysis. Especially now that Achilles is back, as you say, and he and Clytemnestra know that the proposal was a ruse.'

'And I'd say he's run out of options,' said Diomedes. 'The fiction of a wedding is dead in the water now. Both Achilles and Clytemnestra must be outraged. I can't speak for her but we both know how touchy Achilles is in matters of honour. And as attacks on his honour go, this is just about the worst I can imagine. We were quick enough to work out what was really going on when we learned the truth about the wedding. You can bet we're only the first by a whisker if we're the first at all! It won't take any time for people to start working out the truth and if he doesn't offer Iphigenia as a sacrifice to Artemis pretty quickly, he'll have a major mutiny on his hands.'

'Well,' I said, shaken to my core by the fatal danger sweeping so swiftly towards the lovely young Princess, 'he'll have to do some really quick thinking. As we learned from Karpathia herself, the sacrifice and the funeral will both take place on the night of the new moon when Artemis' bow is drawn in the sky itself and her footsteps walk close to the earth.'

'We'll need some quick thinking and fast action too,' said Odysseus decisively. 'You!' he pointed at me. 'Get back to your post outside Agamemnon's tent and keep your ears sharp. I want a detailed report on what the High King is planning to do next!'

iv

'So it was lies! All of it!' Clytemnestra snarled as I eased back onto the dry grass outside the High King's tent, took out my lyre once more and made a show of tuning it, which was just as much of a ruse as Agamemnon's message about the wedding. 'You wanted Iphigenia here because of this madness with the Goddess. Were you really thinking of sacrificing her? In exchange for the life of a stag? A *stag*?'

'It was a sacred stag,' the High Priestess said. 'It had golden horns…' Agamemnon's voice trailed off in a way I had never heard it do before.

'Sacred foolishness!' snapped Clytemnestra. 'Even Artemis isn't vengeful enough to demand the life of a child in exchange for that of a stag!'

'There was a priestess too…'

'Gods give me strength! You killed a priestess *as well*? Had you run mad?'

'It was an accident,' the High King's tone was almost that of a sulky child. 'The stupid girl threw herself in front of the stag just as I fired!'

'So you concocted this pack of lies to get your beloved daughter here so you could kill her to appease the Goddess. A princess in exchange for a priestess!'

'Yes! Or Artemis would chain up the winds and we would never get to Troy. And it breaks my heart! How could it not? I love the girl more than anyone else alive. And yet the curse is happening! Don't you see? Can't you feel? Has there been a breath of wind since you got here? No! And I can tell you it was just as dead calm during all the days before you arrived. And, I suspect, Artemis is by no means standing idle – she is sewing discord through the armies. If we do not move soon then all is lost! They may even turn on us and kill us into the bargain. We have to act or we are likely to die! And the only way we sail for Troy is if Artemis releases the west wind.'

'No matter what the cause,' growled Achilles. His continued presence in the royal tent came as a surprise, especially given the tone of the conversation between husband and wife so far. 'No matter what the cause, you used my name to bring the princess here. That touched on my honour. You and your lies have put me in a position where I must behave as though I really have asked for permission to marry her. Therefore you, Kalkhas, or anyone wishing to lay violent hands on her, even to offer her to the Goddess in the hope it will break the curse, will have to kill me first.'

'Ha!' sneered Clytemnestra. 'You'll need your entire Argive army to do that, husband!'

'But of course,' said Achilles, his tone inflexible, 'if you bring your Argives I'll have to bring my Myrmidons. Furthermore, the Myrmidons are by no means friendless. A confrontation that begins between you and your Argives and myself with my Myrmidons will tear the entire army into two warring factions. And if that happens, we won't stop until both of the sons of Atreus are with the gods up on Olympus – or with Hades in the Underworld.'

'There you have it,' spat Clytemnestra. 'Civil war. And the gods alone know how long you have to think of a way out of it!'

*I know how long*, I thought. You have until the new moon rises like Artemis' bow in the sky.

Then, utterly unexpectedly, a new voice entered the conversation. 'Father. Mother.' Said Princess Iphigenia. 'I cannot allow the entire Achaean army to go to war with itself over me. I could not bear it if one royal hero were to die, let alone the fifty or more you have assembled with their armies here. In what set of scales does the life of one young girl weigh more than the lives of so many?'

'In the scales Menelaus is using,' said Achilles grimly. 'Because he weighs the recovery of his runaway bride against the lives of all the men you would protect, Princess. It is a gallant gesture, Iphigenia, and a noble sacrifice. But no matter how content you are to make it, the weight of my honour still sits in the balance beside you. I cannot allow you to offer yourself any more than I can allow the High King or his soothsayer to accept your offer. Be warned Agamemnon. I will kill the man who touches her whether he has an army ranged behind him or not.'

Having delivered that ultimatum, Achilles came stalking out of the tent and strode off down towards the black ships and the Myrmidon camp. I waited a few more moments, then I followed him down to the shoreline but this time I kept well back.

***

'Hades take the pair of them!' said Odysseus when I reported back aboard *Thalassa* and found him still deep in conversation with Diomedes. 'Agamemnon for his cowardly stratagems and Achilles for his overweening pride! A grain of truth and an iota of humility is all it would have taken. Did you overhear anything else?'

'I heard Achilles leave and saw him start off down the hill. Then Clytemnestra took Iphigenia into the women's quarters. And Agamemnon sent for Kalkhas. That was all. I left and came straight here.'

'Well done,' said Odysseus. 'You have discovered a great deal that is of vital importance. Now we must try and use what we have learned to rescue these two fighting cocks from the situation they have put the entire Argive army in!'

'But it's not just them,' I said. 'It's the Goddess as well. Were she a scrap less vengeful; were the Oracle a jot less rigid in passing down Artemis' terms...'

'Or,' said Diomedes, 'was the High Priestess just a little less inflexible in enforcing them...'

'Indeed,' said Odysseus pensively. 'Indeed! The Oracle and the High Priestess must bear some responsibility too.'

'The only one who appears to be entirely blameless in all of this is Ikaros,' I said. 'He has done nothing but try to help the investigation and to protect me from a range of dangers, both human and super-human.' The memory of the huntsman standing at the dead girl's feet dressed in his acolyte's tunic and his mourning wreath came close to bringing tears to my eyes. But then my ripple of emotion was overcome by a real wave. All of a sudden, *Thalassa* stirred. The deck beneath us

169

lifted and the hull around us canted onto a new angle before it settled once again. 'What was that?' wondered Diomedes, a less experienced seafarer than Odysseus or myself. 'It's a spring tide,' answered Odysseus, apparently thinking nothing of it. 'The water's higher than usual.'

'What is a spring tide?' queried Diomedes.

'The tide will be higher than usual for the next couple of nights,' I told him. 'Like the changes in the weather, it's something to do with the new moon.'

'And it's a new moon tonight, is it?' he asked.

'No,' I said thoughtlessly. 'The moon has been dark – or almost dark – for a night or two already. It's just about to rise with just the brightest new edge showing.'

But then I realised what I had said. I looked across at Odysseus and found him looking fixedly at me. 'It *is*,' he said quietly. 'It's the first sign of the new moon tonight and I had overlooked the fact, fool that I am. Too much focus on the winds and nowhere near enough on the tides! We have only a few hours to put things to rights or we are all lost!'

'But where do we start?' I asked.

'Good question,' grated Odysseus. 'We'll start at the top. I need to talk to Agamemnon.'

The three of us dropped onto the sand. As we did so, I turned and glanced back at the bay. The water was the same intense blue as the sky but it was streaked with white like the feathers of cloud high above. Most striking, however, was the fact that it was creeping higher and higher up the slope of sand with each succeeding wave. The hawsers running from *Thalassa*'s forecastle to the great stakes hammered int the ground were beginning to flex and groan. Then I turned and followed Odysseus and Diomedes as they went hurrying up the beach. As I did so, it struck me just how much of the afternoon I had spent sitting outside the High King's tent. The sun was almost low enough to be shining straight into my eyes from amongst the treetops cresting the ridge. As I hurried after the others I tried to calculate how much time we had before the golden globe vanished entirely behind the Groves of Artemis.

We arrived at the High King's tent, only to find it deserted except for a couple of guards and a confused-looking Achilles with Patroclus at his side. 'They're all gone,' said the Prince of Phthia.

'Where is the High King?' demanded Odysseus, turning to the nearest guard.

The guard he was talking to looked at us, his expression one of extreme nervousness. 'Majesties,' he said, 'of all the kings and princes here, the High King ordered that you should not be informed.'

Odysseus stood silently for a moment, his mind clearly racing. 'He's gone to the Temple,' he said. 'He's planning on completing the ceremony before you can stop him, Achilles. Before any of us can stop him in fact!' He looked up at the sky, frowning. 'I suspect we'll never make it up there by moonrise if we go on foot. Achilles, the chariot you won in the wager a while ago, where is it?'

'Beside the stables where the horses are in Aulis, much like yours,' said the Prince of Phthia.

'Good!' said Odysseus. 'We might still have time to reveal the truth and stop this tragedy without you having to reach for your sword to defend the princess or your honour. Let's go!'

We left at a run, without further hesitation. Achilles and Odysseus were far fitter than I was of course. While I huffed and puffed, they talked. Their conversation was brief. But it turned everything I thought about the case so far on its head.

'Reveal what truth?' asked Achilles.

'That this has never had anything to do with the Goddess,' said Odysseus. 'That it has everything to do with the vengeance of broken-hearted parents mourning the thoughtless murder of their daughter.'

'The priestess Nephele, you mean?'

'Precisely. Nephele, passed off as a foundling raised by an

elderly couple living in Aulis.' We arrived at southern gate as Odysseus said this. 'Their house is a little way down that street,' he continued as we raced into the agora. 'I visited it this afternoon with my rhapsode's father who could teach Agamemnon a thing or two about duplicity, but who could not conceal the truth from me. Nephele was High Priestess Karpathia's daughter.'

## V

My stunned gaze travelled between Odysseus and Achilles as Diomedes and Patroclus roused the stable hands and brought the chariots out. 'But I was brought up here,' I puffed. 'How is it that I knew nothing about Nephele's true parentage?'

'It's not the sort of thing the city fathers wanted bandied about,' said Odysseus. 'Your father was still being very guarded about it when he showed me to their house and I began to test the truth of the matter. The Temple, the Oracle and the High Priestess bring travellers to the shrine, who in turn bring wealth to Aulis. Almost as much as trading does. Your father and his council couldn't afford to risk a scandal.'

'But you were certain that the child Karpathia brought here saying she had been found in the Groves of the Goddess was in fact her own child?' I demanded, scarcely able to believe it.

'Yes,' said Odysseus simply.

'But who is the father?' I asked.

Everyone went silent, then Odysseus answered, 'The answer to that lies at the heart of the problem, of course, and it explains everything – but in a dangerous new light. Come along. I'll tell you as we go.'

Diomedes led out Odysseus' chariot.

'We'll have to hurry,' I warned as Achilles climbed into the chariot he had won during the race on the beach to stand beside Patroclus who was holding the reins of the strongest pair of horses, ready to go. I climbed aboard Odysseus' beside Diomedes and continued, 'It's almost sunset and time for the curfew,' I warned.

Neither the Captain or Achilles said anything, so I babbled on as the chariots thundered side by side through the emptying streets. 'It's the first sign of the new moon tonight. The weather often changes at new moon. Karpathia says it's also the time the Goddess is closest to the earth, with her silver bow curved in the sky. That's why they're completing Nephele's funeral rights with a funeral pyre tonight. I suppose Kalkhas will be saying that the sacrifice must be made tonight as well. The princess dies as the moon rises then both she and the priestess go to the arms of Artemis, who will unchain the winds again.'

'Odysseus flung a few words over his shoulder. 'You were right about the new moon. The weather's on the change. Can't you feel it? I can even smell it,' said the master mariner.

'We have to hurry,' said Achilles. I nodded. His honour was at stake.

Fortunately, the horses on both chariots were well rested and full of running. We made it to the western gate just as it was beginning to swing shut, but a shout from the golden Achilles stopped the process and we were out at the very moment the sun set, thundering side by side up the road to Thebes as the sky in front of us flamed and bled, looking out for the left-turn that would take us to the Temple of Artemis. It seemed that the broken-hearted Agamemnon had forbidden the army to attend the ceremony. Clearly only the royal generals Agamemnon could trust had been invited to witness Kalkhas performing the final act of surrender to the will of the Goddess. Even so, a slow river of soldiery was oozing up the hill, overflowing into the sacred woodland, leaping out of the chariots' way as Diomedes and Patroclus each bellowed a warning. 'So,' said Achilles. 'Nephele's other parent…'

'It was Ikaros,' answered Odysseus. 'He gave up his life as

a successful, well-respected hunter and became a servant of the Goddess at first to be with Karpathia and later to be near Nephele as well. Why else would he do such a thing? They must have been such a contented little family living under the hand of the Goddess until the fatal day that High King Agamemnon went hunting.

'It seemed that Nephele's murder was almost incidental to the Oracle who pronounced the Goddess' judgement. But of course it was central to everything Karpathia and Ikaros did after that. Ikaros found his daughter's body and the place the stag was killed. But neither he nor Karpathia could discover who had fired the fatal arrow. Not even when Karpathia confronted Agamemnon personally - both his wife and his brother agree that one of his greatest talents is barefaced lying. In the immediate aftermath of that failure, she saw me and, knowing something of my reputation, decided to enlist my help. Which, of course, I gave, unaware at that moment that the High King himself was the man we were seeking. He however shared his guilty secret with three others – Menelaus, Kalkhas and Oikonomos his steward – the latter because he needed to dispose of the stag. Menelaus advised him to send the first message to Mycenae and he did so, though he told you nothing about it of course, Achilles.'

'Then he had second thoughts,' nodded the Prince of Phthia. 'And he sent the second message. The one that Sophos carried.'

'We reckoned Menelaus had Sophos killed,' I said. 'He was the one who wanted the matter settled most urgently so his ships could sail to Troy and recover Helen for him.'

'But now we have a different suspect with a different motive,' said Odysseus. 'Ikaros wanted the message stopped because he wanted the princess here in order that her father and mother could feel the pain and loss that he and Karpathia felt.'

'Is that so?' I asked, my mind a whirl. 'The princess's sacrifice has nothing to do with the Goddess, the weather or the winds?'

'Nothing. So Achilles and we can stop the whole tragic mess without actually upsetting the Goddess or condemning Agamemnon's thousand ships to an eternity becalmed off Aulis. As we've already observed, the weather's on the change with the new moon in any case.'

'Then of course we have to stop it at once,' I said.

'What do you suppose we're doing now?' grated Odysseus. And as he spoke, Diomedes swung the chariot in the tightest possible turn beside Patroclus and we were galloping side by side through the Groves of the Goddess towards her Temple, the funeral pyre and the sacrificial altar.

***

'So,' said Diomedes as the horses settled and he could relax his grip on the reins, 'the actions we have been seeing as the hand of the Goddess were in fact the stratagems of grieving parents bent on revenge?'

'I believe I can prove the likelihood,' said Odysseus. 'I suspect they worked out that Agamemnon was guilty even before I did so myself. And if the plans they began to put in place as a consequence seem a little convoluted, consider that they, a priestess and an acolyte at a lowly provincial temple, were trying to enact vengeance on the most powerful man in Achaea. Not only that, but a man who stands at the head of the greatest army ever assembled, and that army is all camped less than a stadion away from where they live.'

'I hadn't thought of it,' said Diomedes. 'But when you put it like that, their predicament is clear.'

'As is the plan, though they adapted it as things went on. First, they enlisted the help of the Oracle who made her pronouncement about the anger of the Goddess and the only way to escape it. The weather helped them there, as did the fact that we sailors who know about such things were in very short supply in Agamemnon's army. And the High King was already at loggerheads with your father and the city elders, lad – the only other reliable source of maritime information.

Apart from me, there's really only Nestor who can read the weather accurately and he was far too fascinated by the stories of the Goddess herself and his similar past experiences to exercise any practical reasoning.

'So, they enlisted my help and attached Ikaros to my little crew. They began to spy on Agamemnon and Menelaus as well as upon us and the progress we were making. Our young rhapsode here had proved what a simple task that can be – the sons of Atreus are used to living in citadels buttressed with cyclopean walls. They do not think to lower their voices in leather- and linen-sided tents. So Ikaros and Karpathia learned of Agamemnon's first message and all seemed well. They waited for me to unmask him, hoping to watch him become trapped by the Oracle's pronouncements, rendered helpless by the will of his armies. But he sent me away because he realised I was getting too close to the truth. The stag was consumed, its gilded antlers a bribe to ensure Oikonomos' continued silence. The second message was sent. And another set of players entered the game.'

'This sounds complex,' said Achilles, who was noted for physical rather than mental prowess after all.

'Not really,' Odysseus answered. 'We know that Karpathia and Ikaros wanted Iphigenia here so they could get their revenge. But Menelaus wanted her here too by that stage because he believed the Oracle. Unless the girl died, he would never recover his wife, his honour or his standing as the second most powerful king in Achaea. Just as his brother turned to Palamedes for support, so Menelaus turned to Aias. Neither man was made privy to what the sons of Atreus were actually doing, but they followed their orders and helped each-other on occasion. So when Ikaros shot poor Sophos from the cover of the bushes on the right side of the road to Thebes, keeping well clear of the Groves of Artemis on the left of course, the wounded man fell at the feet of the Rat and his companion hiding there at Aias' orders as Menelaus had commanded. They cut his throat and tried, unsuccessfully to remove his head as Menelaus or his cohort Aias must have demanded. Ikaros vanished as they completed his task for him.'

'But the Rat and his assistants did not vanish,' I took up the story. 'They kept a close eye on me and when they realised the High Priestess was using me to look in detail at Sophos' death – because, I suppose, she wanted to know more about who had started interfering in her plans – they decided that I was the next rhapsode who needed his throat cut. But,' I hesitated, trying to clear my thoughts. 'You have been saying that the Goddess did not interfere in any of this – that it was all Ikaros, Karpathia and the Oracle. And yet the Goddess did interfere. She sent her great bear to crush the Rat's partner in crime and that saved my life.'

'I cannot disagree,' said Odysseus. 'But I have to observe that the Goddess' apparent interference on your behalf gave Ikaros some very useful ideas. He must have smuggled in the snake that killed the Rat in the end; he somehow mimicked a boar and almost gutted Oikonomos. Getting rid of enemies in ways that further established the personal involvement of Artemis all served very effectively to convince everyone of her supernatural involvement and make this end even more inevitable.'

'They have not destroyed Agamemnon,' said Achilles, impressed, 'but by carefulness and cunning they have made Agamemnon destroy himself!'

'Not if we can help it, Majesty!' I said, my imagination filled with visions of Princess Iphigenia with her hazel eyes, her full lips, her red hair. And her pale throat cut wide by Kalkhas' sacrificial knife. 'Not if we can help it!'

vi

I had no sooner said this than I realised how hopeless our mission might be. We had no stake in the funeral of poor Nephele beyond what her devious parents seemed to have arranged for Agamemnon and Clytemnestra. Agamemnon and Menelaus, however, seemed dead set on fulfilling the demands of the Goddess, ignorant though they were that those demands were entirely bogus. And they appeared to have brought many of the leading generals of the army to witness the fatal act. Many of whom, starting I assumed with Palamedes and Aias but supported by many of the others who were themselves impatient – or who knew their armies to be so – would stand beside them even if it came to blows. But, I consoled myself, no matter who stood against us, I was in the company of the most fearsome warrior alive and three others who ran him a close second. I had paid little attention to the matter before now, but these thoughts filled my mind as we approached the temple precinct. I glanced at the kings and princes I was riding with. Achilles and Patroclus were in armoured breastplates and backplates, though they were both bareheaded. But they were both armed to the teeth as the saying is. Diomedes and Odysseus were wearing no armour, but both of them had swords and daggers at their belts. And each chariot was carrying half a dozen spears.

We galloped into the precinct side by side and reined to a stop. The whole place was deserted but the last light of day showed us a crowd of people on the stepped slope behind and above the temple. Or, I realised as my vision cleared, two crowds – one gathering round the lower level where Nephele's funeral pyre had been built just out from the foot of the modest cliff leading up to the higher level where Kalkhas' helpers had built the altar on which Iphigenia was doomed to be sacrificed. The crowd gathering on the higher level seemed to be wearing much more metal than the group around the funeral pyre. Once again I rehearsed how lucky I was to be in company with four of the deadliest warriors alive.

Both the funeral and the sacrifice were due to commence when the new moon began to rise across the greenish turquoise sky, which was beginning to darken towards sapphire as the shadows of night gathered relentlessly. The crowds seemed dark and amorphous but as we arrived, so the people organising them began to light lamps and little golden earthbound stars leaped into life before those in the sky could reflect them. There was a rumble of expectant conversation which seemed to come and go as the wind gusted gently through the pine-trees on the high western ridge.

Achilles stepped down from his chariot. 'Right,' he said, easing his sword in its scabbard. 'Let's go.'

'Spears?' wondered Patroclus.

'I think not,' advised Odysseus. 'We're not up against the Trojans yet.'

'Good point,' said Diomedes. 'Sweet reason and sharp swords it is.'

We set off up the slope, pushing through the soldiers sluggishly gathering there in expectant groups. Our urgent footsteps soon brought us level with the first plateau where Nephele's pyre stood almost as tall and as long as a man but wider than three men with the figure of the poor girl indistinctly pallid in her white wrappings on the top of it. As we passed, I recognised the strange smell from the cold room where we had seen her laid out that morning. 'What is that smell?' I asked.

'Bones,' answered Diomedes.

'More specifically, antlers,' said Odysseus.

I paused, squinting. And there indeed were the golden antlers that had seemingly cost Oikonomos his life, arranged in a kind of crown around the dead girl's head. 'But there is so much wood available,' I said. 'Why burn bones?'

'Tradition,' said Odysseus. 'It makes the whole matter a sacrifice as well as a funeral. The Goddess should be doubly gratified.'

'If she actually cares about human life and death,' I said. 'Even on the night she's supposed to come closest to the earth.'

'Let's not risk upsetting her, though,' suggested Diomedes as we strode on past the pyre and the crowd of priests, priestesses and acolytes gathered around it waiting for the moment it would be lit. I shrugged; he was right: better safe than sorry when you're dealing with easily irritated Olympians. I could see neither Ikaros nor Karpathia, but a tall woman I assumed to be the Oracle stood immediately behind the antlers, her figure swathed in formal robes, the light from her lamp-flame gleaming on the gold and illuminating the sleeping face of the dead priestess. Then we were on the slope that led to the upper level where Kalkhas had had his sacrificial altar built. This was a two-tier arrangement, standing high so that everyone would get a clear view of the proceedings. The altar itself was a waist-high table as long and as wide as a man but it stood on another, wider, pediment that reached knee-high above the dry, scorched grass. This was where Kalkhas stood in his soothsayer's robes and formal headdress, with the intrepid sacrifice lying still on the altar-top with her grieving parents beside her. All the other witnesses were gathered round expectantly in rows several men deep and this was where our real problems stood assembled.

*\*\**

We formed a wedge as though we were indeed going into battle. Achilles was at the point with Patroclus behind one shoulder and Diomedes behind the other. I suspected Odysseus would have been right behind him too had he not positioned himself a little further back to keep a protective eye on me. 'Stop!' bellowed Achilles in a voice rivalling that of Stentor our herald. 'The man that touches the princess dies!'

Everyone turned and looked at him. Even Iphigeneia sat up and stared. He was a sight worth looking at, of course, with his golden hair and golden armour almost as bright as a lamp-flame in the gathering gloom. And there was the fact that he was challenging the better part of fifty kings and princes ranged against him. Long odds, even for the greatest warrior alive.

Odysseus stepped forward. 'Agamemnon,' he called, 'You need to stop this now. You are not the plaything of a vengeful Goddess, you are the victim of a devious trap. The dead girl awaiting funeral down there is the daughter of the High Priestess and her lover Ikaros. Ever since she died they have been working to trick you. First into admitting that you did the deed yourself. Secondly into bringing your most beloved daughter here to sacrifice her to Artemis – who neither knows nor cares about our petty human doings. And thirdly that you and Queen Clytemnestra suffer the grief and loss that Karpathia and Ikaros suffered when you killed Nephele whether or not you did so accidentally.'

Agamemnon swung towards Kalkhas, who stood at the head of the altar with the sacrificial knife gleaming and ready in his hand. Iphigenia was between them, dressed in sacrificial robes, her face a pale glimmer marked with huge dark eyes.

'That's not right,' bellowed Agamemnon. 'That can't be right!'

'The King of Ithaka is mistaken,' said the soothsayer, his voice ringing through the thickening shadows. 'I have spent many hours talking with Artemis' oracle in the temple and I know the will of the Goddess. Were she not at the root of this, how would the wind be stopped? Were she not at the root of this, how would her animals be working her will amongst us? Her bear, her snakes, her boar, all avenging the death of her stag?'

'The wind is not stopped,' called Odysseus. I realised then that he was claiming the attention of the High King, the Soothsayer and all the rest while Achilles and Patroclus began to ease themselves surreptitiously round the outer edge of the assembled witnesses, moving relentlessly towards the altar. And they clearly needed to do so, because both Agamemnon and Kalkhas had spoken. Neither of them could afford to back down now. Their pride was worth more than the life of a girl, even a daughter and a princess. Any loss of face would be witnessed by the men they planned to lead into a war. Men whose absolute trust, therefore, could not under any circumstances be compromised.

I had reached this stage in my reasoning when there was a strange kind of roaring sound from behind me. I turned, as did everyone around me, and looked down. Nephele's funeral pyre had just burst into flames. Shocked breathless, I turned and looked up into the darkening bowl of the sky. And there indeed was the thin white bow of tonight's new moon climbing over the southern horizon.

'Stop!' came Achilles' stentorian voice. We all swung back. He and Patroclus had indeed managed to get around the assembled kings and princes. As the Prince of Phthia spoke, so he stepped up onto the raised section of the altar beside Kalkhas, his sword gleaming in the lamp-light. Everything froze for a heartbeat, then another figure appeared. At first I thought it must be Patroclus for it appeared at Achilles' side. But no. This figure was wearing no armour over the white tunic; no helmet, but a mourning wreath. It was Ikaros, and he was wielding the strangest weapon I had ever seen. At first I thought it was a scythe, with its long handle and angled blade. 'Ah,' said Odysseus. 'That explains Oikonomos.' And I realised that what I had supposed to be a blade was in fact the tusk of a massive boar. I had seen helmets made of boar-tusk, but never anything like this. 'Perhaps we should have brought a spear or two after all,' concluded the King of Ithaka.

Ikaros swung his strange weapon at Achilles and only the prince's reflexes saved him. He got his sword up in time to save his face, but the point of the thing still scored the golden breastplate, Ikaros recovered instantly and swung the weapon again. Agamemnon took Clytemnestra by the arm and they both stepped down off the altar. Iphigenia lay flat again, well clear of both sword and tusk. Patroclus appeared, ready to join the battle but Achilles called, 'Leave me! Guard the princess!'

\*\*\*

Achilles leaped off the altar's raised surround and the assembled kings fell back to give him fighting room. And they needed to do so, for Ikaros' makeshift scythe looked sharp and deadly – and it required a good deal of space to deploy it as he was doing now. He swung it fiercely round his head as he advanced and the warlike kings all stepped further back. Achilles fell into his fighting stance but he had no helmet, spear or shield. His only advantage, it seemed, was that incredible speed of his. Once again the vicious tusk swung in towards Achilles' unprotected head. He raised his sword. Ikaros instantly changed the angle of his attack, The tusk sliced down towards the prince's thigh. He skipped back, only just avoiding the blow and I realised with a lurch that although he was wearing armour, he had neither greaves nor thigh-guards. As Ikaros was recovering from the near-miss, Achilles glanced over his shoulder and established for himself something that I only just realised as I watched him do it. A couple more passes like that and the prince would be over the cliff-edge close behind him. Ikaros saw it too and approached once more, swinging his strange weapon in a circle in front of him, driving Achilles back another couple of steps. The Prince of Phthia was dangerously close to the edge now and every eye in the place was focused upon him and his strange opponent. Every eye except Odysseus'. 'Patroclus!' bellowed the captain. 'Look out!'

I tore my eyes away from Achilles and swung round. I was just in time to see Kalkhas tumbling backwards off the altar step and another figure rearing in his place. It was all over in a heartbeat, and yet I seemed to see every detail as though Time itself was standing still. The figure in Kalkhas' place raised its arm. The dagger in its fist gleamed wickedly in the lamp-light as it plunged down. 'No!' screamed Queen Clytemnestra. Patroclus reacted instinctively, I suspect even before he realised precisely what was going on. His sword swung round in a vicious arc. Its blade took the strange figure right across the throat. The head seemed to spring from the shoulders of its own accord as a massive fountain of blood followed it upward then downward as the headless body collapsed backward. And in that strange flickering golden light of the lamps and the torches, the head of Karpathia, High Priestess of Artemis landed on the breast of the princess she had just killed with the expert stroke of someone adept at making such sacrifices.

Although he had his back to her, Ikaros screamed at the instant Karpathia died, his agony every bit as intense as if he had witnessed the entire episode. Though, to be fair, he must have known how the desperate act would end. His scream of agony became a roar of madness and he charged at Achilles swinging the tusk straight at his opponent's face. Achilles threw himself backwards. His shoulders hit the ground at the edge of the low cliff. Smoke and sparks from Nephele's pyre writhed and eddied around and above him. Ikaros' charge towards him did not slow, on the contrary, the screaming man accelerated, the strange weapon raised for the killing stroke. But even as he began the downstroke, the apparently helpless man beneath him was in action. With a speed that was scarcely believable, Achilles raised his sword, held in both his fists. By sheer muscular control, he tore his shoulders back up off the ground, curling himself like the tail of a scorpion, with the bronze sting of his swordpoint uppermost. The blade entered Ikaros' belly just below his belt and vanished up into his chest. The boar's tusk hit the ground well behind Achilles' head, chopping a clod of dry earth off the edge of the cliff. Ikaros' legs weakened, for he was dead, but the great charge he had launched himself into carried on. Achilles rolled back, straight arms rigid and unyielding. Ikaros went over the top of his would-be victim, over the edge of the cliff and, taking Achilles' sword with him still buried to the hilt, he crashed down into the blazing pyre beside his dead daughter.

There was a moment of silence, broken only by the sobs of

Iphigenia's distraught mother, then the pines along the top of the ridge bowed, as though the Groves of the Goddess were saluting her High Priestess for completing the sacrifice after all, or the thin white curve rising in the night sky over her temple beyond. And a strong west wind began to blow.

Maybe the Goddess is walking near the earth after all, I thought, and she accepts her debt as paid in full.

Or maybe the weather simply changes with a spring tide and a new moon after all.

# SOURCES

Major sources:
Iphigenia in Aulis Euripides tr George Theodoridis
Iphigenia (1977 film) dir Mihalis Kakogiannis
The Iliad new Penguin edition tr Martin Hammond
Also tr Caroline Alexander
Also tr E V Rieu
Also tr George Chapman
The Odyssey tr E V Rieu
Online etc: Michael Wood In Search of Troy (BBC)
Ancient History Documentary The True Story of Troy An
Ancient War.
The Trojan War & Homeric Warfare
The Trojan War - Myth or Fact
The Truth about TROY
Great Battles: Was there a Trojan War? Recent Excavations at
Troy
The Trojan War Episode 2: Weapons and Armour During The
Trojan War

Academic sources:
The Book of Swords Richard Francis Burton
Greek Mythology – The complete guide
Bulfinch's Mythology Thomas Bulfinch
The War That Killed Achilles Caroline Alexander
The Wooden Horse – The liberation of the Western mind from
Odysseus to Socrates Keld Zerundeith
The Wooden Horse - Some Possible Bronze Age Origins - I.
Singer (ed), Luwian and Hittite Studies.

Creative sources:
The Silence of the Girls Pat Barker
The Song of Troy Colleen McCullough
The Song of Achilles Madeline Miller
Troy Adele Geras
NB All 'Songs' are based on Ancient Greek poems adapted
from various translations.

CPSIA information can be obtained
at www.ICGtesting.com
Printed in the USA
BVHW041956010821
613374BV00016B/660